Granite Publishing Presents

Love Notes

#2

To Echo The Past

To Echo The Past

By Marcia Lynn McClure

Published by:

Granite Publishing and Distribution, LLC
868 North 1430 West
Orem, Ut. 84057
(801) 229-9023   Toll Free (800) 574-5779
Fax (801) 229-1924

Cover Design and Art: Tammie Ingram
Layout: Triquest Book Services

ISBN: 1-59936-0004
Library of Congress
 Card Control Number: 2005933590

Printed in the United States of America 2005

To Tina Brynn,
In remembrance of those happy moments....
Always.

CHAPTER ONE

Brynn Clarkston gazed despondently through the parlor window and out into the dusty, abandoned street. It was a warm, bright summer day but her spirits were cool and blue. She abhorred this small town to which her family recently moved. She was a stranger to everyone; they were strangers to her. There were few young people her age. She missed her friends in the east. There were no grand shops, no scented bakeries, no park with a band playing in the gazebo, no automobiles, no opera, no medicine stores with soda counters. She sighed as she reflected on these memories of the colorful, musical city her family had left behind. She had no choice but to accept this brown, lifeless town. She had to call it home.

Her father, Richard, was an educator, and well respected in his profession. He relinquished his position at the university to become a teacher at the local school in this isolated western town. He had explained to his wife and children that he harbored a craving for adventure and felt the West would provide it. What choice was left to Brynn, his eldest daughter? None.

Brynn did not complain when the family arrived to find the township and its people a little primitive compared to others she had known. These people had a drawling manner about their speech, and very few of the women were properly corseted.

"Heathens," her Aunt Rebecca called them.

Brynn knew the people in town and the farmers and ranchers who lived on its outskirts were honest, hard-working folks for the most part. However, as Mr. Beevis Bellmont walked past and flashed his rotting-toothed smile at her, she wondered if any of the honest, hard-working folk were in the least bit attractive.

Sighing heavily once more, Brynn deserted her post at the window and went to the mirror standing in one corner of the room. Another heavy sigh escaped her lungs as she studied her own reflection. She was tall with a slender, yet pleasing figure which humbly boasted the perfect curves for an ideal feminine form. Her hair, dark, long, and brilliantly soft, was accentuated by red highlights. The blue of her eyes was equaled only by the pure hue of the heavens.

Brynn, being blessed with an overabundance of modesty and a pleasing lack of vanity however, saw none of these sought after attributes as she gazed at her reflection on that warm summer day.

"Darling..." Brynn's mother said as she entered the room. She immediately noticed the dissatisfied expression on her daughter's face. "You're looking uncommonly lovely today," she continued.

Ophelia Clarkston was a woman above others. She was the matured version of her daughter in every physical aspect, but possessed the knowledge akin to a woman of experienced years and wisdom.

Brynn sighed, knowing her mother was trying to dispel her negative thoughts. "Thank you, Mother," she said. "But you'd say that if I were Medusa herself."

Brynn studied at her mother for a moment wondering how such a beautiful woman could be so blissfully happy with her lot. After all, hadn't her mother been one of the most beloved diva's of her time? She broke the hearts of many admirers when she retired from the opera to wed the man she'd fallen in love with…Brynn's father.

Brynn studied her mother's flawless complexion and brilliant blue eyes, and she wondered how it would feel to possess such beauty.

"True," her mother admitted. "But, you're not. Venus more likely."

"Mother, I detest this dreary, dry town!" Brynn sighed again, going once more to the window.

"You only need to adjust, darling. Make some friends! You never go out." Ophelia smiled with understanding. "This very minute...why don't you go out for a stroll. Wander down to Mrs. Johnson 's store and pick out some cloth for that new dress I promised you."

Brynn smiled. "Very well. Perhaps the fresh air will do me good."

———•———

Fifteen minutes later, Brynn crossed the threshold of the general store.

"Good morning, Mrs. Johnson ," she said to a jolly elderly woman sitting in a worn chair behind the counter.

"Hey there, Brynn. Yer lookin' particularly purty this morning," Mrs. Johnson said.

Brynn was curious about the elderly woman. She had heard talk of Mrs. Johnson's being well into her seventies. Yet, she was quite alert, friendly and able-bodied.

"Thank you, but I'm afraid I'm feeling far from pretty today." Brynn smiled when Mrs. Johnson shook her head in disagreement. "Mother sent me to choose cloth for a new dress. Do you mind if I have a look?"

"Not at all, Peach. Let me know when you find somethin' you like and I'll put it back for you until your mama comes in."

"Thank you," Brynn said with a smile. She liked the older woman. Her eyes always sparkled as if she harbored a secret knowledge that amused her.

Half-heartedly Brynn began browsing through the bolts of cloth on a shelf. Finally deciding on a pretty cream colored calico with tiny blue flowers, she picked up the heavy bolt of cloth, and returned to the counter. Holding the bolt of cloth to her face she asked, "Well, what do you think, Mrs. Johnson? Is this the one for me?"

As she raised her eyes to look for Mrs. Johnson, her heart skipped a beat and nearly stood still. Just inside the door stood an extraordinarily handsome man! Her grip loosened on the heavy bolt of cloth and dropped to the floor landing on Brynn's right foot.

"Ow!" she exclaimed. She was horrified when the vision of pure masculinity stepped forward to retrieve the bolt of fabric and set it on the counter.

"That there musta hurt, miss," he said. He squatted before her and brazenly took her injured foot in one hand. "Do ya think it's broke?" he asked.

Brynn could only shake her head in silent response as the blue of his eyes captured the blue of hers.

"Glad to hear that," he said straightening up. He towered over Brynn, and extended his right hand in greeting.

Brynn took his hand and he shook it firmly. "I don't believe I've met you before...Miss...Miss..."

"Brynn Clarkston," she sputtered.

"Miss Clarkston," the young man repeated. He flashed a dazzlingly white set of teeth as he smiled. "I'm Michael. Michael McCall. My family's been ranchin' 'round here since right after the war 'tween the states. I don't get into town often...but maybe I oughta make a point of it."

Brynn blushed as he winked at her. "We just moved here from back east," she explained.

"Well now...that's right refreshin'," he chuckled. "My mama will be durn near to splittin' a gut with excitement when she finds out there's new folk in town. Both of my auntie's will, too, I reckon."

"You...you have a lot of family around here?" Brynn asked. She desperately wanted to keep the conversation going with this young man.

"Shoot, yeah!" he confirmed exuberantly. "This place is crawlin' with McCalls."

Brynn smiled. It seemed there were actual civilized human beings nearby, after all–attractive ones! "How encouraging," she replied.

"Hey, Mrs. Johnson," he said. "Why didn't you tell me there was a new...and right purty young lady in town?"

The old woman chuckled. "I figured you'd find out for yerself soon enough, boy. You sniff 'em out quicker than anybody."

Michael looked back to Brynn and smiled. Still talking to Mrs. Johnson he asked, "I come in for some liniment and witch hazel."

Brynn found it difficult to look directly at him. His eyes were probing, as if he could see her innermost thoughts.

"Been breakin' them horses again have ya?" Mrs. Johnson asked.

Brynn looked to the floor. Michael McCall bent his head toward her until she was forced to meet his gaze once more. He smiled and nodded, still talking to Mrs. Johnson.

"Heck, yes! Them boys need to be broke if'n we're gonna get 'em sold. It makes Mama awful nervous to have Daddy doin' it, you know."

At last, the handsome cowhand turned to the elderly woman. "S'pose ya better throw in a new shirt, too, Mrs. Johnson. I done ripped this one near to shreds. Mama will have a fit when she sees it."

Brynn hadn't noticed before, for she had been so entranced. But, now she looked to see his shirt untucked from his Levi's and hanging open exposing the browned, muscular torso beneath. There were several tears in the garment and one shoulder was blood stained, obviously from a wound that lay beneath.

Gasping at the unexpected sight of a man's bare chest, Brynn reflexively closed her eyes to shade them from it. She opened them again, however, when she heard the amused chuckling of Mrs. Johnson and the young man.

"Ain't used to blood, huh?" Michael McCall asked her. "Don't worry, Miss Brynn, it's just a little ol' scratch." Reaching up he pushed the shirt from his shoulder revealing a painful looking laceration. "Though I don't normally admit to it...I got bucked off and hit the fence. It don't hurt much now."

Brynn looked away. The blood did not make her uncomfortable. The sight of a half-nude man did.

"Let me get those things together for you now, Michael," Mrs. Johnson said. She quickly walked into an adjoining room.

Brynn took a deep breath. She looked up to find Michael smiling at her.

"So, what brings your family out here?" he asked.

Brynn swallowed before answering. "My...my father has accepted a teaching position here."

"He's a teacher?" he asked.

"He was a professor at the university, but wanted to move west. So, here we are," she explained, taking a deep breath. She was aware her hands were wringing her skirt.

"How many Clarkstons are there?" he asked, smiling and taking a toothpick from a small dish on the counter. He opened his mouth slightly, setting the toothpick on his tongue. When he closed his mouth again, the toothpick protruded from one side of his grin.

Brynn cleared her throat and cast her eyes down before answering. His smile was too intriguing! "Five," she answered. "My father and mother, my sister Sierra, my brother Scottie and myself."

"You're the oldest child?"

She looked up at him. "Yes, sir."

He chuckled. "Darlin', I can't be more'n two years older than you now, can I? You call me Michael."

Brynn smiled. "Very well."

He chuckled again and continued. "My mama will like you. It's been some time since she had a conversation with someone so proper. She's darn near nagged herself blue tryin' to get us childr'n to talk right."

Brynn smiled. She was again mesmerized by the toothpick as she watched it slide to the middle of his lips and begin flickering up and down rapidly.

Michael chuckled and took the pick from his mouth. "Nasty habit, I know. But Mrs. Johnson keeps these out here just for us. It's a sight nicer than tobacca, don't ya think? 'Sides...tobacca turns yer teeth all yeller and black. Ain't a girl on this earth that wouldn't rather a man had white teeth than yeller. Especially come time for sparkin'. Don't you agree?"

Brynn cleared her throat and again muttered nervously, "Yes. I suppose that's true."

"Here you go, boy," Mrs. Johnson called as she returned. "Witch hazel for all them bruises yer bound to have collected on your seat. Liniment, and a nice white shirt. Don't go tearin' this one up tomorrow, you hear me?" she said smiling.

"No ma'am, I won't," Michael said, taking the items from her. "In fact, why don't we save Mama the trouble of havin' a fit today, Mrs. Johnson." Before Brynn could attempt to shade her eyes or turn away, Michael McCall stripped off the tattered shirt and threw it into an old garbage basket sitting nearby.

"Heathens!" Aunt Rebecca's voice echoed in Brynn's mind as she stared at the shirtless man before her.

The thought quickly passed through her mind that maybe heathens weren't so bad, provided they all looked like Michael McCall and not Beevis Bellmont.

"I better get back," Brynn gasped anxiously. This man was truly unsettling. Retreat was the only alternative. "My mother will be in to pick this up as soon as she can, Mrs. Johnson ," she said as she turned to quietly leave.

"Now, don't rush off on account of me, Miss Brynn. You and Mrs. Johnson go on about yer girl talk. Thank you, Mrs. Johnson," he said. "Our little secret?" he added with a wink.

"Yes, boy," Mrs. Johnson chuckled. "Now git!"

"And what a pleasure to meet *you*, Miss Brynn," he said, smiling. "I'm sure we'll bump into each other now and then." He turned and left the store.

Mrs. Johnson dropped her voice to a whisper when he was gone. "He's a fine young man, isn't he? Good lookin', too. He's his daddy over and over except for them blue eyes. He gets them from his mama. Young Michael McCall's a might more pleasin' to look at than a mud fence, ain't he?"

Brynn was unable to deny he was truly a dream, so she nodded, blushing as she did so.

"I knew his grandma, Maggie McCall, real well. Real well. She died a few years back, but his mama and daddy, Jackson and Malaina McCall, live on the main farm. He has two uncles with families that live on their own properties. There's Baker and Charlotte McCall...they got six kids and Matthew and Mary McCall, they got five. Michael's got a brother and two sisters. I bet young Annie is about yer age. She's sixteen, I think. You can't dodge the McCall clan 'round here no matter how hard you try."

Brynn nodded and whispered, "He's very polite. Charming, actually."

Mrs. Johnson smiled. "He took right to ya, didn't he?"

Brynn shook her head and sighed. "I'm not the kind of girl he'd look twice at, Mrs. Johnson," she whispered.

"Well, Sugar," the woman chuckled in a whisper. "He looked more'n twice just while you were standin' here a showin' me this cloth."

Brynn smiled. "Well…I better get back! Now, you'll save this cloth until Mother can come in, won't you, Mrs. Johnson ?"

"Of course, Brynn. Of course."

———•———

The day brightened considerably since Brynn first left the house. As she walked towards home from Mrs. Johnson 's store along the dusty street she didn't mind the dry smell of soil as it filled her lungs. Something began to whisper to her that perhaps living in the small western community wouldn't be so terrible. Hadn't he said that the place was simply "crawlin'" with

McCalls? That in itself gave her hope. Of course, she didn't really care about any other McCalls. One, the one she had met, was more than enough.

"Mother!" Brynn called as she entered the house through the kitchen door. "Mother! I've something to tell you."

"In here, darling. Come quickly. We have our first visitors," Ophelia called from the parlor.

Brynn walked quickly to greet her mother but stopped abruptly when she saw that her mother sat in the company of three women. One woman was a very unique beauty. The dark-haired, blue-eyed woman rivaled her own mother's loveliness. A lovely blonde woman was present and next to her another dark-haired woman who somewhat resembled the first one.

"This is my eldest daughter, Brynn," Ophelia said, motioning for Brynn to greet the women.

"Hello. How do you do?" Brynn greeted with a forced smile.

The three women returned the greeting with smiles.

"Brynn, these lovely ladies have come to welcome us to town. This is Charlotte McCall."

The second dark haired woman extended a tiny, gloved hand to Brynn. Brynn took her hand for a moment, smiling.

"And this is her sister-in-law, Mary McCall," Ophelia said as she indicated the blonde woman.

"Hello," Brynn said, taking the second woman's hand.

"And this is Malaina McCall. She's Mary's sister-in-law and Charlotte's sister and sister-in-law! Oh, it's all so confusing ladies! However do you keep track of everyone?" Ophelia asked.

"Hello, Brynn," Malaina McCall greeted, taking Brynn's hand.

Brynn could only smile. The realization was washing over her that this was the mother of the handsome vision she had only just met. As she looked into the woman's beautiful blue eyes, she recognized their similarity to her son's.

"You're lovely, my dear," Malaina commented. Then looking from Brynn to her mother and back ,her smile widened and she added, "The image of your mother."

"Actually, she looks a great deal like her father," Ophelia added.

"I'm so very pleased to meet you, Mrs. McCall," Brynn said, awestruck by the woman before her and who she represented. "I've only just come from Mrs. Johnson 's store where I met your son, I believe."

"Which one, dear?" Malaina asked.

"Michael," Brynn answered.

Malaina giggled, and Brynn found it delightfully intriguing that such a graceful woman would have girlish laughter.

"Oh, yes! My Michael. He's been into the general store, has he? Was he appropriately dressed or not, my dear?"

Brynn thought it an odd question. "Well, he...he..."

Charlotte spoke. "He bought a new shirt, I've no doubt."

"Why, yes," Brynn exclaimed, astonished.

"And some liniment to boot, I reckon," Mary added.

"Yes. Yes he did," Brynn confirmed.

Malaina turned once more to Ophelia. "Let me explain, Ophelia. My charming son takes after his father. They break horses as part of their labors. I've no doubt that Michael has soiled, if not utterly destroyed, yet another shirt in the process. He thinks I'm innocent to the fact that he spends part of his earnings almost weekly on new shirts, attempting to hide the fact he's been roughed up by some wild stallion he's determined to break."

"Michael's very cute, isn't he?" Mary unexpectedly inquired of Brynn.

"Well...well..." Brynn stammered.

"Of course he's handsome," Malaina answered for her. "He takes after his daddy." Malaina smiled beautifully then. "I've a daughter just about your age, I think. Annie. She's sixteen."

"I'm seventeen, yes," Brynn confirmed.

"Oh wonderful! The two of you will get along beautifully. She looks like me. Fortunately, she lacks some of my most unbecoming flaws. And Mary and Charlotte both have sons and daughters that are near your age."

"How many children do you have, Malaina?" Ophelia asked.

"Four. Only four. But they're wonderful. Michael is the eldest, he's twenty-two. Then Robert, he's twenty. The girls are next. Margaret is nineteen and Annie sixteen," she answered.

"How delightful!" Ophelia sighed.

"Tom and I have six children," Charlotte said. "We've three sets of twins in the litter. Two boys, twins that are twenty-two. Two girls, twins that are nineteen and a boy and a girl, twins that are fifteen."

"My goodness, Charlotte!" Ophelia exclaimed in amazement. "Do you lean toward triplets, Mary?"

"No. Ours are singles. Our eldest is twenty-two as well. He has the same birthday as

Charlotte's boys. Then we have a daughter twenty-one, a daughter twenty, a daughter nineteen, and a son fourteen," Mary explained.

Ophelia released a sigh of astonishment. "I'm surprised that the town hasn't been named McCall with all of you living here."

"Do you have other siblings, Brynn?" Mary asked.

"A younger sister, Sierra, and a younger brother, Scottie," she answered. "Both terribly bothersome."

As the three ladies giggled Ophelia smiled, too, scolding, "Now, Brynn. Be kind."

"How charming," Malaina said. "But, we shouldn't keep you any longer, Ophelia. That dashing school teacher husband of yours will be livid if he finds a group of giggling old crones in his parlor when he returns."

"Dashing! Father?" Brynn questioned, for she saw him as her tender, caring protector— her beloved parent.

"Yes, of course, 'dashing', my dear," Charlotte agreed. "You've got his eyes, too. Yes, I do see the resemblance you referred to, Ophelia."

"We met your father this mornin', Brynn. He insisted we not waste another moment in coming to meet your dear mother. And I'm glad we didn't," Mary explained. "Oh,

Ophelia...we're so glad to have you and your family here! It will be wonderful to have a friend in town."

"Yes," Malaina agreed. "Now, Matthew and Mary are having a barn raising the end of this month. We'll let you know exactly when."

Mary and Charlotte nodded their heads enthusiastically.

Malaina continued, "You simply have to come and meet everyone!" Then turning to Brynn she said, "Annie will be thrilled to meet you! And, if I know my Michael, he'll be looking forward to your family attending."

———•———

"I don't think I've ever seen a more beautiful woman, Mother," Brynn said. It was evening, and the family was seated at dinner.

"Malaina McCall? Yes, she's a rare beauty. I tell you, Richard, I would've thought her not a day over twenty-five had she not told me her age," Ophelia said.

"Quite a story there, too, I understand," Richard Clarkston said as he took a bite of mashed potatoes.

"What? You mean the way she met her husband?" Ophelia asked.

"Yes. Extraordinary story," he answered, taking another bite.

"What story?" Sierra, Brynn's ten-year-old sister, asked.

"Well," her father began, swallowing his third bite of potatoes. "It seems that Jackson McCall, that's her husband, simply found her in the wilderness one day. She was weakened from exposure and had no memory." The family waited impatiently as he helped himself to a large bite of bread and butter. "To condense the tale, Mrs. McCall, Malaina, was a native New Orleanian and some horrid villain was stalking her. It all met in the middle one day, it seems. Jackson and his two brothers, all three honored graduates of West Point, I might add, dueled to the so-called death. Triumphant, Jackson McCall married his beloved Malaina. Seems there was something or other about a renegade band of Indians as well."

"Indians? Really, Daddy? Indians!" seven-year-old Scottie squealed.

"Indians?" Ophelia asked, unsettled at the thought.

"Yes, Ophelia, Scottie. Indians. It seems some violent leader type took Malaina hostage at some point. Her gallant hero helped the beast to expire and saved the fair maiden.

I think she even had to extract a poisonous arrow from his shoulder."

Brynn smiled, completely enchanted by her father's telling of the tale. He had such a way with the retelling of stories. "You're making it up, Daddy," Brynn giggled. "Renegade Indians? Poisoned arrows? What did she do, Daddy? Cut him open and drain out the poison?" Brynn smiled. Richard Clarkston could really invent a tale.

"No. No. I believe she extracted the arrow and then proceeded to suck the poison from the wound. Yes, yes. That's it. No, wait...yes, Mr. McCall pulled the arrow from his own shoulder and used it to impale the renegade. Yes, that's how it went."

"Oh, Daddy. How nauseating! And at dinner!" Sierra whined.

"It's the truth. Young Grant McCall, their nephew, related the tale to me only yesterday. Truly."

"He's embellishing, Daddy. Surely!" Brynn said.

"No. I think not. In fact, they tell me that the villain from New Orleans who was stalking Mrs. McCall is buried in the cemetery just outside of town. You've seen it, Brynn. The one we passed on our excursion last Saturday."

"Well, what was his name then—this man who tried to abduct her? We can all go just after dinner and look him up, can't we?" Ophelia suggested. "It's a beautiful evening and it still will be light enough."

Richard Clarkston chewed a piece of meat thoroughly before responding. "Yes. That would be nice, dear. As for the man's name...Collin something. Collin Mereaux. That's it. We'll all go then, just after dinner."

Brynn believed her father's story did indeed have a basis, but to imagine the beautiful Malaina McCall sucking poison from someone's shoulder? Impossible!

"Well, I'll be," Ophelia exclaimed as she stood before the tombstone. "Look here, Brynn. 'Collin Mereaux.' That's all it says."

Brynn gazed at the slab of granite lying on the ground. Indeed, the name was there. But, only a name and a date. No epitaph.

"Why should it say more, dear? He was a villain as the story goes," Richard reminded them all.

"Do you think it's true, Daddy?" Sierra asked. "Do you think someone really tried to kidnap Mrs. McCall? Do you think Mr. McCall really fought bravely for her, winning her in the end? Oh, how romantic," she sighed.

"I bet it was bloody," Scottie interjected. "Nice and bloody."

"Scottie! How gruesome!" Ophelia scolded.

"He's a man above men, they say," Richard stated.

"Who, dear?" Ophelia inquired.

"Why, Jackson McCall, dear. They say he can break any horse alive."

"I think you spend entirely too much time listening to gossip, Richard darling."

"They say he's a handsome brute, too," Richard added, smiling affectionately at his wife.

"Not as handsome as my brute," Ophelia whispered.

Brynn smiled contentedly as she watched her father place a loving kiss on her mother's forehead and hug her securely in his arms. They were deeply in love—even after so many years. It was evident every day of their lives.

Brynn looked at the tombstone again. She thought how horrid it all must have been. How 'bloody' as Scottie had put it. Suddenly she was very curious to set eyes on this Jackson McCall—the legendary man who rescued and wed the beautiful Malaina, the handsome man who was the father of Michael McCall.

As if in answer to her thoughts, a low greeting came from behind.

"Hello there. You must be the Clarkston family."

Brynn turned to see Malaina and Jackson McCall standing before her and her family. She was astonished at the uncanny resemblance this man bore to his son. His temples were graying and his eyes were green, but this was Michael McCall's very image.

"Oh, good evening," her father greeted, extending a hand toward the other man. "Yes. I'm Richard Clarkston. We've met your lovely wife. Am I correct in assuming that you are Mr. Jackson McCall?"

"That's me," the handsome man confirmed. "We rode out tonight to freshin' the flowers on my mama's grave. She's right over here. I see you're givin' ol' Collin the twice over."

Brynn blushed, humiliated at being caught hovering over the villain's grave.

"Yes," her father confirmed. "Young Grant was relating the fascinating story to me yesterday. I retold it tonight at dinner only to find four sets of very skeptical eyes staring at me."

"It's all true," Malaina said, standing next to Brynn and gazing down at the tombstone. "Horribly true."

"Even the Indians and the arrow part?" Sierra asked, her blue eyes widening.

"Yes, sweet thing. Even the arrow part," Malaina answered smiling sweetly at the child.

"Dang right! Especially the arrow part, Sugar," Jackson McCall added. He quickly unbuttoned his shirt pulling it aside to reveal a large, blackish scar on one shoulder.

"Jackson McCall!" Malaina scolded. "Button that shirt! You're as bad as the boys!"

"Naw! They wanted to see it, didn't you kids?" he asked directly to Scottie.

"Yeah!" Scottie whispered moving closer. "It's so ugly!"

"Scottie!" Ophelia reprimanded.

"It is, ain't it, boy?" Jackson agreed. "But don't you think my Malaina was worth it?"

Brynn giggled as Scottie glanced briefly at Malaina and shrugged his shoulders. Jackson chuckled and tousled the boy's fair hair. "It's good to have new folks in town. And you," he said turning his attention to Brynn.

Immediately, her hands dropped to her skirt and began viciously wringing the garment. "Yes, sir?" she responded.

"Michael told me he met a member of your family today. Judgin' from his description, I'd say it was you."

"Yes, sir," she confirmed.

Jackson McCall grinned knowingly and chuckled, "Had his shirt off, didn't he?"

Brynn blushed slightly, but was relieved from responding when Malaina took hold of her husband's arm tightly and said, "That's enough, Jackson." Smiling she looked to Ophelia. "It was so nice to bump into you out here. We simply must get together for a chat. I mean that, Ophelia."

"We will, Malaina. We will," Ophelia assured her. "We'll be off and leave you to your visit," she said.

Jackson and Richard shook hands and then Jackson again turned his attention to Brynn. "Next time you meet up with Michael, don't feel like ya gotta go on blushin' so. Though, I did have the same effect on his mama and still do for that matter whenever I take off my..."

His words were silenced by his wife's lovely hand as she tightly clamped it over his mouth.

"Forgive him, Brynn dear. 'The apple doesn't fall far from the tree' they say," Malaina whispered and winked.

———•———

"Charming couple," Brynn's father commented on the walk home. "Charming."

"Yes," Ophelia agreed. "There's something very unique about them. They're deeply in love."

"It's a blessing, dearest—unfortunately, many aren't endowed with it." Taking his wife's hand in his own, Richard added, "Thankfully, we are."

"I think he's the handsomest man I've ever seen in my entire life," Sierra sighed.

"You're only ten, Sierra," Scottie reminded his sister.

"So? Did you see the way he caressed her cheek with the back of his hand? He's a truly romantic man."

Scottie grunted in disgust indicating his sister's remark had upset his stomach.

"Scottie! That's enough," Ophelia scolded. "You're terribly quiet, Brynn. Whatever is your mind working on now?"

"Oh nothing. I was just thinking what a nice family they seem to be." She neglected to add she had also been thinking about the ruggedly handsome face that had first appeared before her in the general store earlier that afternoon.

CHAPTER TWO

Brynn was longing to see Michael McCall's face again. As one week turned into two, Brynn hadn't seen him since the day in Mrs. Johnson's store. Furthermore, the weather had turned gray, gloomy and wet.

The rain turned off and on for hours at a time as if to tease and titillate the townsfolk. It would stop, the clouds would disperse, the sun would shine enough for everyone to dash out into the brightness of the day. And then, to the despair of all, the clouds would quickly gather, drowning out the sun's rays, and the monotonous sound of falling water would recommence.

It was on such a day that the weather tricked Brynn into venturing out. She decided if her moods were dampened by the weather, then those of Mrs. Johnson certainy must be as well. She pitied the elderly woman who had no one. The story going around was that her only child, a daughter, died tragically years ago. When her husband had passed on, she was left lonely and without any family. The Clarkston children tried to fill her lonely void by visiting her as often as possible.

Brynn had found that Mrs. Johnson possessed a wealth of historical knowledge about the town and its inhabitants past and present. She enjoyed their visits and hoped each time she entered the store she would find Michael McCall needing liniment.

Half way to the store rain began to pound the earth. In moments Brynn's teeth started chattering from the cold wetness.

As she dashed into the store, Mrs. Johnson quickly rose from her chair behind and went to the girl.

"Brynn! Dear child. For pity's sake! What would drag you out into this storm? You're soaked to the skin!" the woman exclaimed.

"I wanted to visit with you. It looked like I would have plenty of time to get here when I started out," Brynn explained.

"You'll catch your death, Sugar," Mrs. Johnson mumbled as she began drying Brynn's face with her apron. "Run back to the other room now. I've got a fire goin' and I'll have you some warm cocoa in a jiffy. Just let me finish helping ol' Beevis pick out a shovel," she instructed.

Brynn nodded and smiled. She liked the store's back room. It was warm if the weather was chilly, and cool when hot. To Bryn, it was the coziest place on earth. Pictures were scattered on the walls. And ferns hung from the ceiling. The furniture was worn and comfortable. It was simply a pleasant place.

Upon entering the room this day, however, Brynn was startled to see someone else there. Sitting in a large chair before the fire, his bare feet propped lazily on a hassock, sat Michael McCall.

"Miss Brynn!" he exclaimed. "Fancy meetin' you here! And on a day like this. Got caught in the rain too, I see."

Brynn wanted to turn and run. She realized what she must look like—a cat having narrowly escaped a drowning in a bathtub.

"Yes, caught in the rain," she mumbled.

"Well, here now," he said, arising from the chair. "Sit yerself down and warm up. You'll catch yer death."

Again, he was shirtless. She shook her head quickly and forced her gaze to his face.

"No, no, no," she stammered. "I'm fine. Really!"

"Nonsense, darlin'. Yer soaked to the bone. Now take my seat. I'm warmin' up now." Stepping forward, he took her hand and guided her to the chair.

Brynn sat down stiffly and stared nervously into the fire. Her intention was to keep her eyes off his magnificent physique.But to intentionally thwart her determination, Michael sat down abruptly on the hassock directly in front of the chair.

"I heard you met my mama and daddy," he said.

She looked into his grinning face, and its expression of utter mischief.

"My mama's a real beauty, ain't she?"

Brynn nodded again and smiled.

"Did you like my daddy? He said he showed yer little brother his arrow scar. It's one of his nastiest,though. I'm gettin' my own here and there," he said. Brynn could only smile in response and he continued, "Mama says yer only seventeen. Is that right?"

Brynn suddenly felt ashamed of her youth, but she nodded her head.

"Dang! I coulda swore you was at least nineteen." When Brynn only continued to smile, he asked, "You cold, darlin'? You ain't gettin' a fever already are ya?"

When Michael McCall put his hand to her brow to check for fever, Brynn felt she might melt into a puddle of warm water right there before him and the fire. His mere touch provoked feelings and sensations which Brynn had never before experienced. She wondered at that moment if she did, indeed, have a fever. She was instantly warmed. At the same time, she felt nervous and agitated.

"Hmm. You feel fine," he said. "Still, I reckon we best get you cozy." Before Brynn could move out of his way he stood up, leaned forward and reached for an afghan, which was folded over the back of the chair. As he leaned over, his body was only inches from her face. She smelled the aroma of leather and bacon. She turned her face to one side for fear the bareness of his chest might actually touch her. The thought flushed through her mind that her mother would absolutely perish if she were to see her daughter in such an improper circumstance.

Michael grabbed the cover and dropped it sloppily over her lap.

"There. Now you can talk to me," Michael said with a grin. He reached over to a small bowl that sat on a nearby table. Taking a toothpick from it, he promptly placed it in his mouth. He dropped himself onto the hassock, rested his arms on his knees, and looked at her expectantly. "Tell me somethin' about yerself."

"For instance?" she was able to verbalize at last.

"For instance...are you likin' it out here—as compared to where ya come from, I mean?"

Brynn paused and then said, "Yes. It's very nice."

"Yer lyin'." He chuckled and his grin spread further across his face. "Yer lyin' like a dog, darlin'."

Brynn cast guilty eyes to the floor. Then meeting his amused eyes, she corrected herself. "I'm adjusting," she said, momentarily distracted by the toothpick rapidly flickering up and down again.

"Now why don't you like it? We got all a body needs out here. Food, water, air...McCall boys," he added with a twinkle in his eye.

Brynn felt a full smile sweep over her face.

Michael chuckled, "Now...that's what I like to see. That purty little mouth of yers curled up at the corners." Reaching out, he tweaked her cheek. Brynn was deflated at receiving a gesture meant more for a child.

"I hear yer mama was some big fancy singer back east 'fore she married yer daddy," he said, leaning back toward the fire. As the muscles in his upper body tensed to support the weight of his position, Brynn gulped, feeling uncomfortable again.

"She...she was a diva with the New York opera," she awkwardly explained. "She retired when she married my father."

Michael raised his eyebrows with a look of being impressed. "Remind me never to sit next to her in church. I'd send her screamin' down the isle."

Brynn smiled and muttered, "I doubt that." Again, she found herself mesmerized by the trick his mouth played with the toothpick.

"Impressive, ain't it?" he said with a chuckle.

Brynn smiled. "I admit, I can't do it."

"I'll teach ya sometime," he whispered, winking.

Instantly Brynn was agitated. This man was far too attractive! She felt unsure of herself, unable to stay calm. She rose from her chair and allowed the cover to fall from her lap as she turned and walked to one of the pictures hanging on the opposite wall.

"Is this her daughter?" she asked. The photograph was of a lovely young woman. She immediately regretted her inquiry when she sensed

Michael had risen and was standing directly behind her.

"Yeah," he whispered. "That's Elizabeth. See this one?" He pointed to another in which Elizabeth stood with a very handsome young man.

"Her wedding photograph," Brynn remarked, noting the veil and bouquet.

"Yep. That's my Uncle Baker. She was his first wife, before Charlotte. Elizabeth died very young."

"How sad," Brynn whispered. Then realizing Michael's uncle now had another wife, she felt stammered, "I mean...at the time."

Turning, she saw Michael wore an amused grin as he looked down at her. "I know what ya meant, Miss Brynn," he chuckled once more. He looked past her to the photograph. "I think Mrs. Johnson likes to look at me as the grandbaby she never had."

Michael's gaze fell once more to Brynn. For a moment their eyes locked in an instant of mutual wonderment. Brynn watched as his eyes narrowed slightly. The toothpick momentarily ceased its fluttering.

"Why do I make you so nervous?" he whispered.

"I'm...I'm not nervous," Brynn stammered.

She watched anxiously as he removed the toothpick from his mouth and moistened his lips with his tongue. "You're lyin' again," he chuckled. Brynn stood paralyzed as he bent to her ear. His mouth hovered. She could feel the warmth of his breath on her neck. She thought her heart might burst from her bosom when he whispered, "I 'spose you'd slap me smack 'cross the face if I tried to steal a kiss from you, wouldn't you, Miss Brynn?"

"Yes," she whispered in a shaky, uncertain voice.

He leaned closer. Instinctively she put her hands out, and felt her palms flush with the bareness of his chest. Quickly, she withdrew only to find herself replacing them when he continued to move closer. The feel of his warm, smooth skin alarmed her. When he at last pulled back, she felt as though his warmth burned through her hands, traveled the length of her arms, and settled in her cheeks.

"You got a mighty cute blush," he said with a chuckle. "And I'm a pantywaist for teasin' ya like that and not followin' through." He placed his one hand gently under her chin, tipping her head upward to look into his face. He then placed the toothpick back into his mouth, and moistened it. Removing it, he tenderly pricked her lip with it.

When she gasped, he slipped the small sliver of wood onto her tongue. Reflex caused Brynn's mouth to close. Michael smiled and tweaked her cheek once more. "I'll teach ya that trick another day, darlin'," he said. "I gotta get on home 'fore my mama thinks I'm drowned, which, by the way, I will be if Mrs. Johnson comes in here and finds me flirtin' with you like this."

Brynn started to turn away. She needed to escape! He caught her arm, and when she looked up to him, his mirthful grin was gone. He wore an expression of extreme sincerity.

"I *am* sorry, Miss Brynn Clarkston. You've just formed a weakness in me, that's all," he whispered. Shaking his head, he released her and went to get his boots from near the fire.

"Oh, Michael!" Mrs. Johnson exclaimed as she entered the room. "You ain't ridin' off already are ya, boy?"

Michael looked up at the old woman as he pulled on his socks. "I gotta get home 'fore I get myself in trouble, Mrs. Johnson ."

"Well, boy, ya ain't hardly dried out yet."

"Yeah, well, it's too awful warm in here for me today, thank you," Michael chuckled. Quickly, he pulled on his boots. As he put on his shirt he said, "Thank you, Mrs. Johnson . It's always so nice to visit with ya." Brynn began wringing her skirt as he walked toward her. "I believe that's mine, darlin'," he said, plucking the toothpick from her lips and placing it in his own mouth once more. "Now you ladies have a nice visit this afternoon, ya hear?" He put on his hat, tipped it and with one last dazzling smile, left.

Mrs. Johnson giggled. Lowering her voice to a whisper, she asked, "Did I leave the two a you alone long enough, honey?"

Brynn cleared her throat and pulled at the collar of her blouse. "Too long, Mrs. Johnson."

Mrs. Johnson chuckled. "He gets under yer skin, don't he, Brynn?" When Brynn only blushed, Mrs. Johnson continued, "He's like a flea that needs scratchin', that one. And he's taken a fancy to you. I can tell."

"He's a grown man, Mrs. Johnson. I'm only seventeen. I'm sure he views me as no more than a school girl still in bloomers," Brynn retorted.

Mrs. Johnson smiled to herself. "Well, you come on over here and have a cup of cocoa with me, Sugar. We'll have us a nice little visit."

Mrs. Johnson talked almost endlessly but Brynn registered little of her babble. Her mind was spinning, reviewing over and over the moments she had shared with Michael McCall in the back room. She could think of nothing but the feel of his breath on her neck, the scent of his body, and the taste of the toothpick he had placed in her mouth.

Some hours later, Mrs. Johnson yawned and said, "I'm tuckered in, Brynn. And you need to be gettin' on home. You tell your mama hello for me, won't you, honey?"

"Yes. Yes, of course, Mrs. Johnson ," Brynn stammered, rising to leave.

Then, at that moment, they heard someone call from the outer room. Mrs. Johnson walked into the store followed closely by Brynn.

"Oh good gravy," Brynn heard Mrs. Johnson mutter gloomily as they entered together. "Help us all, it's Annabelle Barrington."

Brynn looked to see a young woman standing at the counter.

"Oh there you are, dear Mrs. Johnson! Why, you haven't aged a day since I left last fall," the young woman sang out.

"What brings you home, Annabelle?" Mrs. Johnson asked flatly. It was obvious to Brynn that Mrs. Johnson was not excited about this particular customer.

Annabelle laughed coyly. "Why, Mrs. Johnson! I've completed finishing school! Have you forgotten? I only had one year left."

"Went awful fast, didn't it?" Mrs. Johnson mumbled.

Annabelle began looking about the store curiously. "I heard Michael McCall was in here today. Is he still about somewhere?"

Immediately, Brynn felt her own teeth clench and every muscle in her body tense.

"No. No. He's gone on home. He got caught in a downpour and dried out in the backroom with Brynn here," Mrs. Johnson answered. "Oh. I guess you haven't met Brynn have you, Annabelle?"

Brynn didn't miss the mischievous twinkle in the elderly woman's eyes as she reached back, took hold of Brynn's arm and pulled her forward.

"This is Brynn Clarkston. Her family's purty new in town. Brynn, this is Annabelle. Annabelle Barrington."

"No doubt you've heard of me, Brynn. So nice to meet you," Annabelle said, feigning sincerity.

"Hello," Brynn managed through still clenched teeth.

"Well, if he's not about..." Annabelle said, looking around once more as if expecting to find Michael despite what Mrs. Johnson had said. "I guess I'll just float on home. It was so nice to see you again, Mrs. Johnson. And to meet you, um...um..."

"Brynn," Brynn stated.

"Oh, yes. *Brynn*. Odd name, isn't it?" She turned and gracefully floated from the room.

"That one there," Mrs. Johnson began, "That one there is a true and utter pill! Can't stand the girl myself. I was all too relieved when she went away last fall. And, she moons over Michael McCall somethin' awful! It's embarrassin' if you ask me. He don't pay her no mind, though."

"I better get home," Brynn whispered, suddenly feeling depressed.

———●———

The rain clouds seemed grayer and the air damper as Brynn walked toward home. Not that she had expected Michael McCall to really harbor any interest in her. After all, he was a grown man of twenty-two. She was only seventeen. Annabelle Barrington did look the part of the ideal woman. Still, she knew it would be difficult, nearly heartbreaking to have to watch Michael with anyone else. But, hadn't he threatened to steal a kiss? Of course, boys, men were like that. Always teasing. Always breaking young female hearts.

Straightening her shoulders, she drew in a deep breath and said outloud, "I don't care! He's a rogue, that one. There's not a serious bone in that man's body." And through her mind once more she thought of the perfectly formed body he had.

As she entered the house through the back kitchen door, she heard her brother and sister squabbling as usual.

"Mother, Scottie pulled my hair!" Sierra whined.

"Hair? That ain't hair, Mother! It looks like an old rag mop dyed in tar," Scottie sneered.

"Isn't hair, Scottie? Isn't hair? You know your sister has lovely raven hair. Quit irritating her," Ophelia scolded firmly, yet calmly. "Hello, Brynn dear. Dinner is nearly finished. Could you mash the potatoes?"

"Of course," Brynn answered as she opened a drawer to remove the potato masher.

"Did you have a nice visit with Mrs. Johnson?"

"Yes. I got soaked going over, though."

"I hope you dried off sufficiently before starting home. I don't want you catching cold. That reminds me," Ophelia began, "Mary McCall dropped in on me this afternoon and invited our family to something called a 'barn raising' out at their farm the end of the month. Doesn't that sound interesting?"

The announcement startled Brynn and the potato masher clattered to the floor.

"Careful dear. Be sure to rinse it off," Ophelia reminded her.

"What's a barn raising?" Brynn asked, feigning indifference.

"I'm not certain. I guess we'll just have to wait and see. All I know is that I volunteered to bake two cakes. I can't believe I volunteered for cakes! You know the trouble I've been having with this oven. Brynn dear, whip the potatoes nicely when you've finished mashing."

"Your cakes are marvelous, Mother. You've nothing to worry about," Brynn said.

"Anyway," Ophelia continued. "I suppose we better get busy and finish that new dress of yours so you can wear it. Oh, I hear there's a young lady in town just about your age who has returned from Finishing School. Her name is Annabelle Barrington."

Brynn sighed and began attacking the potatoes with the masher. "I've met her, Mother. She and I will not get on together...I assure you of that."

"Well, now how can you know that having just met her?"

"I know, Mother. I know. Please don't force the issue," Brynn pleaded, whipping the potatoes mercilessly.

"Very well, then," Ophelia conceded, recognizing a sensitive subject. "Your father came home at lunch time and it seems there's been another stage held up not more than fifty miles from here."

"That's three since we've been here," Brynn commented beginning to feel a bit insecure. "And they're getting closer, aren't they?"

"It would seem that way," Ophelia answered.

"Daddy says they shot the stagecoach driver clean full of holes!" Scottie expounded.

"Don't exaggerate, Scottie," Ophelia corrected. "He said the perpetrators shot him, that's all."

"I bet he was clean full of holes!" the boy exclaimed again.

"Scottie! You're so gruesome!" Sierra exclaimed with a grimace.

"Children, let's not start that again. I tell you, I'm nearly sick to death of your squabbling today," Ophelia sighed. "Brynn dear...I'm sure those potatoes are sufficiently whipped by now. Run along to the schoolhouse and fetch your father. He's probably got his nose buried in papers and hasn't looked at his watch."

Brynn set the bowl of potatoes aside and left the house. She was relieved to find the weather was being benevolent and the sun was shining once again.

She did find her father feverishly working at his desk in the school house.

"Daddy," she said, startling him.

"Brynn. How nice of you to visit me...I..." Then realizing the reason for his daughter's visit he quickly plucked his watch from his vest pocket and examined its face. "Oh, my. Your mother has sent you to bring me to dinner, hasn't she?"

Brynn smiled and nodded. Her father was so dear—always reading some novel or another, some professor's essay, even the dictionary. She admired his diligence.

"Tell her I'll be along shortly. Just want to finish up these examinations," he said, returning his attention to his work.

"Yes, Daddy." She giggled as she turned and left the small schoolhouse. She wondered as she walked toward home what fascination her father could find in leaving a reputable university and coming to a small town schoolhouse.

"Well, there you are, Miss Brynn," a voice called to her as she was crossing the main road through town.

Recognizing the voice, Brynn immediately remembered she hadn't even run a comb through her hair since she returned half damp from Mrs. Johnson's. Bravely turning to face him, she answered, "Hello, Mr. McCall."

She caught her breath as she saw him. Why was it she always forgot how perfectly handsome he was until the moment he popped up again?

"Dried up purty nice out, didn't it?" he said, coming to stand directly before her.

"Yes...yes it did," she stammered. She began wringing the fabric of her skirt nervously.

The ever present toothpick in his mouth flickered quickly. Brynn wondered for a moment if it were the same one he'd taken from her earlier in the general store's back room.

"I got somebody over here I want ya to meet. Can you spare a minute?" he asked, taking her hand and pulling her along without waiting for an answer.

A young woman stood not too far from where they had met in the road. Brynn knew at once this must be Michael's sister, for the girl was the very image of his mother.

"This here's my sister, Annie," he said as he stopped next to the girl.

"Hi," Annie said and smiled. "Michael says he thinks me and you will get along just fine."

Brynn was enchanted by the lovely girl. "I'm Brynn," she announced.

"He told me," Annie giggled.

There was an uncomfortable silence. Michael finally broke it saying, "Well, looky who we have here. If it ain't Miss Annabelle. I thought you was back east somewheres finishin' yer schoolin'."

Brynn looked away from Annie to see Annabelle Barrington approaching as graceful as silk in the breeze.

"Michael!" the young woman sang. "There you are! I had no idea you were still in town today. And you've brought little Annie with you, too. How sweet."

"Yeah, I'm helpin' Mr. Bellmont break that new colt he brung in," Michael answered, smiling.

"And, yes, we met in Mrs. Johnson 's this afternoon...um...Fynn, isn't it? Odd name," Annabelle said.

"Brynn. It's Brynn," Brynn corrected her.

"My, yes. That's it. Interesting hair dressing, child. You may want to run a comb through it more often," Annabelle said, lowering her voice.

"That there's my fault," Michael interjected. "I mussed it up when I...when I...bumped into her earlier at Mrs. Johnson 's."

Brynn gasped and her mouth dropped open in horror at his insinuative remark.

"Oh, I see. Forgive me, dear...will you?" Annabelle apologized. Quickly, she took hold of Michael's arm and began leading him away.

"You'll lend him to me for a moment, won't you, girls? It's been so long that I've been away. Michael and I must catch up."

"Um...I'll meet you back at the stables in a few minutes, Annie," Michael said. "Don't go runnin' off. Ma will have my hide if you get into any scrapes today."

Then, as Annabelle tugged at him impatiently, Michael took Brynn's hand in his own and shook it firmly. His touch was sensational. Brynn was paralyzed for a moment. "Good evenin', Miss Brynn. Sorry about that...uh...little incident in the general store. Next time I'll be more thorough," he said. As he walked away, Brynn looked to find his toothpick lying in the palm of her hand. The small sliver of wood was still moist at one end from being held in his mouth. The knowledge sent a thrilling shiver through Brynn's being.

"Good riddance," Annie mumbled. "She makes my stomach churn." Brynn looked quickly to the girl who continued to vocalize her opinions. "She's the devil in a girl's face, I tell you," Annie whispered, nodding with affirmation at Brynn. "She's been after Michael since she was walkin'. It just makes me sick." Annie looked expectantly at Brynn. When no response was offered to her remarks she prodded, "Come on, Brynn. You know she makes you wanna shove her in the waterin' trough."

Brynn smiled. She liked Annie's honest forthrightness. "Yes. She does. She's the most obvious fake I've seen in my life."

Annie nodded. "Dang right! Don't worry, though. My brother Michael is the smartest man on this green earth. He knows her ways."

Brynn smiled at Annie who smiled back. Annie giggled and said, "I can tell we're gonna get along right well, Brynn Clarkston."

"I believe so," Brynn agreed. "I was just on my way home for dinner. Do you want to walk with me a ways?"

"Oh, yes! Michael will be forever and a day at the stables and I've been bored to tears since Mama went home earlier. If I had known he was going to hang around so long, I probably would've gone home with her. But then I wouldn't have gotten to meet you yet, would I?" Annie babbled quickly as the two girls began walking together.

"No. I'm glad you've been bored to tears, until now anyway," Brynn said. "You look so much like your mother I can't believe it."

Annie shook her head. "Don't I only wish! I got the color of her hair maybe, but that's it. Now,

Michael...he looks just like my daddy. Don't you think he's just as cute as anything on earth?"

"Michael or your daddy?"

"Well, both of 'em, I guess," Annie giggled. "Don't be shy about it, Brynn. You wouldn't be half normal if you didn't think so." Brynn raised her eyebrows and nodded in agreement. "Do you like it out here? Michael says you're from some fancy city out East? Do you think it's dull and dreary in this little western town?"

"I have to admit to you, I did...at first. But Mrs. Johnson, and your mother and aunts, and you and...well, you give me hope," Brynn responded. "Here's my house. You must come in and meet my mother."

Annie dropped her eyes shyly, "I...I don't know. I heard she was a purty big to do singer way back. I'd feel funny."

"She's just my mother. Now, come on. She'll be offended if you don't."

Brynn opened the front door allowing Annie to enter first. Annie stepped into the Clarkston house and looked about nervously. "Mother? I've brought someone to meet you," Brynn called.

Ophelia appeared from the kitchen drying her hands on her apron. "You've brought company, Brynn? How marvelous!" Ophelia stopped abruptly upon seeing the girl, and Annie fidgeted uncomfortably. "Oh my! You are the very vision of your mother! You must be Annie!"

"Yes, ma'am," Annie answered, dropping a slight curtsy.

Ophelia rushed forward and took the girl's hands in her own. "Isn't she just the vision of Malaina McCall, Brynn?" Brynn smiled and nodded in agreement. "Now you come right on in here and sit down to dinner with us, Annie."

"Oh,   no,   ma'am...I   couldn't possibly...impose...I...my brother will be..." Annie stammered.

"Nonsense. You must stay and meet Brynn's father!"

"Oh, but really, Mrs. Clarkston...I..."

"Come along then and talk to us while Brynn and I finish up dinner, which, by the way, is getting cold. Did you hurry your father along, dear?" Ophelia inquired of Brynn as she tugged at Annie, leading her into the kitchen.

"He'll be right along I would think, Mother," Brynn answered, amused at the silence Ophelia had inspired in Annie McCall.

"Now, sit right here and tell us all about yourself, dear," Ophelia instructed the girl, offering her a chair.

"There's not much to tell, ma'am," Annie sputtered.

"Nonsense! Tell us about life on a farm. Whatever in the world is a 'barn raising' anyway?"

Annie smiled and came to life. Her sweet babbling words spilled from her lips like an infinite waterfall. "Oh! Just the best thing on earth, ma'am. You see, each barn has to have a frame put up first. It really is the hardest part of buildin' a barn. So, folks get together and put up the frame and then there's food and dancin' and just plain fun for the rest of the day and night! It's wonderful! You all are going to Uncle Matthew's for his raisin' I hope."

"Oh my, yes! We wouldn't want to miss something so wonderful!" Ophelia chimed.

"Mama! Scottie is wipin' his nose on his sleeve again!" Sierra whined, bursting through the back door. "It's making me sick. Tell him to stop. He's doing it on purpose!"

"Well, all she ever wants to do is play house, and get rescued by some dumb prince! I hate it and my nose is running. What am I supposed to do, Mama?" Scottie defended himself, bursting in after his sister.

"You carry a handkerchief like a gentleman should, Scottie. Go change your shirt before dinner. I swear, you drive me to lunacy! And Sierra, try playing something Scottie might enjoy, too, once in a while, dear," Ophelia instructed. Sighing, she turned to Annie and added, "You've now met Sierra and Scottie, Brynn's younger brother and sister. Please don't judge us too harshly by their behavior."

Annie giggled as Scottie stopped to stare at her for a moment before dashing off toward the back of the house.

"Good evening, cherished family," Richard announced, entering through the back door. "I see we have a lovely guest. And, judging from the uncanny resemblance, I would guess you would be a McCall?"

Annie nodded and said, "Yes, sir. I'm Annie McCall."

"How very pleasant to meet you, Miss McCall. I'm Richard Clarkston. I assume you are above the age that would require you to attend school?"

"Yes, sir. I finished last year," Annie assured him.

"Ah. Then I won't have to inform the truancy officer, will I?"

Annie looked stunned and her face paled. "No, sir."

"Only jesting, my dear. Merely jesting," Richard chuckled, kissing Ophelia affectionately on the cheek.

"The potatoes are far from hot now, dear," Ophelia scolded.

"Ah, cold, hot or warm...it matters not to me. Potatoes are simply the staff of life. Don't you agree, Miss McCall?" Richard chuckled.

A knock on the door sent Annie leaping to her feet. "That's Michael and he's gonna be madder than an ol' wet hen at me for sneakin' off!"

"Nonsense, dear," Ophelia assured the girl. Going toward the door she added, "We simply can't send the two of you home without a decent meal! Whatever would your mother think of me then?"

As Brynn watched her mother open the door she drew in an anxious breath. Could it really be Michael McCall come to her very own house to collect his sister? As her mother exclaimed "Oh my!" upon opening the door, Brynn knew that it must, indeed, be Michael. "Oh my!" Ophelia exclaimed again as she turned and looked at Brynn curiously. "I'd guess you're Mr. Michael McCall."

"Yes, ma'am," came the answer in the deep voice all too familiar to Brynn. As he stepped into the parlor, Ophelia looked to Brynn again, raising her eyebrows, obviously impressed by who had just entered her home. "I'm a...lookin' for my sister, Annie. I thought maybe she might a come on home with Miss Brynn," he explained, removing his hat immediately.

"Why, yes she did. And I've told her that the two of you simply must stay for dinner," Ophelia told him.

"Hello, young man. I'm Richard Clarkston," Brynn's father said, stepping into the parlor and extending his hand to Michael. "We're very glad to meet you. You seem to have an exceptional family, my man."

"Thank you, sir," Michael said, taking Richard's hand and shaking it firmly. "We'll be gettin' outta your hair now, Mrs. Clarkston."

"Nonsense, Michael. You and Annie cannot possibly leave before having a bite to eat with us," Ophelia insisted, shutting the front door behind him. "Now come along and sit down to dinner. We would love to hear more about you and your family. Brynn is simply too quiet and never lets us know a thing." Ophelia looked to her daughter knowingly as she motioned for Michael to follow her.

"You're very kind, ma'am. But Annie and I do need to be gettin' on home. We wouldn't want to impose anyhow," Michael argued.

"Now listen here, young man," Richard interceded. "You aren't wanting my dear wife to have her feelings hurt, are you?"

"Well, no sir, but..."

"Then it's settled. You'll have dinner with us," Ophelia stated.

As Michael entered the kitchen behind Ophelia, Annie broke into nervous chatter. "I just walked home with Brynn, Michael. Honest! And Mrs. Clarkston was so insistent that I..."

"I ain't really dressed for dinner, ma'am," Michael said to Ophelia, though he glared at Annie.

Brynn smiled. The shoe was on the other foot, so to speak. It seemed that fate had placed Michael in the uncomfortable position this time. She dropped her eyes as he looked at her and smiled.

"You're dressed wonderfully, Mr. McCall," Ophelia assured him. "Now you sit right down. Richard, darling, would you call Sierra and Scottie? Why don't you sit between Annie and Michael, Brynn dear. They know you best."

Brynn's smile left her face immediately as Michael said, "That's dandy with me. How about you, Annie?" As Michael winked at her, Brynn looked quickly to her mother to see if she had detected the flirtatious gesture. She sighed with relief when she saw that her mother was busy taking the roast from the oven.

Brynn looked blankly at Michael as he pulled a chair away from the table and motioned for her to sit in it.

"For goodness sake, Brynn. Don't gawk at a gentleman when he knows his manners," Ophelia scolded.

Brynn allowed Michael to seat her at the table. He repeated the same service for Annie, then sat on Brynn's right.

"You must be Michael!" Scottie exclaimed, entering the room and staring blatantly at the male guest.

"Yes, sir. That's me," Michael chuckled, offering a hand to the young boy.

Scottie shook Michael's hand. It was obvious to Brynn that her little brother was intent upon impressing Michael.

"I heard you and your daddy get all manner of injuries breaking horses. I heard between the two of you, you've lost enough blood to fill a lake!" Scottie exclaimed in a whisper.

"I'm Sierra," Brynn's younger sister said, approaching their guest with her beautiful blue eyes as wide as lakes themselves. "You're very handsome, Mr. McCall."

Brynn wanted to sink into the floor and disappear at the brazen remark uttered by her sister, until she noticed the slight pink that colored Michael's cheeks.

"Shucks, Miss Sierra. What are you butterin' up an ol' goat like me for?" he said, tweaking her nose.

"You got any big, nasty cuts on you, Mr. McCall?" Scottie asked.

"Oh, one or two. But it wouldn't be polite to show 'em to you just now, boy," Michael chuckled. "Maybe later," he added in a whisper.

"Oh, boy!" Scottie exclaimed, excitedly taking a seat next to his father.

As the meal continued, Brynn listened intently to the questions her father posed to Michael and the answers he offered in return.

"Exactly what kind of farm do your father and uncles run, Michael?" Richard asked.

"Well, sir...Uncle Baker raises beef cattle. Uncle Matthew takes care of the wheat and alfalfa. My daddy runs the horse end of things with a little alfalfa thrown in," Michael answered. "It's a good life. My daddy and both his brothers were West Point graduates, but they're glad they went back to farmin' and ranchin' 'stead of goin' into the military permanent."

"I think your mother and your aunts are simply jewels!" Ophelia commented.

"Yes, ma'am. And ain't little Annie here the spittin' image of my mama?" Michael asked.

"My yes!" Ophelia agreed. "Do you like farm life, Annie?"

"Yes, ma'am!" Annie assured her. "I can't imagine not havin' fresh air and carin' for animals. You'll have to come out and spend some time with me at our place, Brynn."

"That's a right good idea, Annie," Michael agreed. Brynn gasped slightly as she felt his leg brush against hers for a moment. She looked at him suspiciously, but he only smiled and took a bite of potatoes. "These are right good mashed potatoes, Mrs. Clarkston."

"Aren't they, though?" Richard agreed, serving himself a second helping.

Brynn found it impossible to eat. She could feel Michael, smell him, sense him with every ounce of her body and spirit. His arm brushed hers once and she jumped nervously.

He chuckled and dropped his voice so the others, who were all involved in a conversation about the recent stage and bank robberies in the state couldn't hear. "Don't be so jittery, darlin'. You'll give us away." Then she felt him step lightly on her foot with his boot and he winked at her.

She couldn't resist smiling at him, for he was adorable. And polite! She couldn't believe his polished manners. She felt guilty for expecting any less from him.

Some time later, as they all were finishing their meal, Annie muttered to Brynn, "Mama's gonna wring my neck. Michael probably will too once we're gone."

"No. You're mama will understand that you couldn't possibly refuse dinner here! My mother would have been hurt," Brynn assured her.

"I hope you're right, Brynn," Annie sighed.

"Mrs. Clarkston, this was a dandy of a meal. I tell you, you could give my mama some right serious competition," Michael chuckled as he folded his napkin and placed it neatly beside his plate.

"Oh, must you rush off?" Ophelia pleaded.

"Yes, ma'am. I'm afraid so. Mama's gonna be a worryin' as it is. Not so much about me...but she worries about Annie bein' out."

"Well, thank you so much for joining us. You two drop in any time you're in town. Do you hear me?"

"Yes, ma'am," Annie answered sweetly. "If you really mean it, that is."

Ophelia laughed, "Of course I mean it, Annie! You're welcome anytime."

Richard started to stand as Michael rose from his chair. "No need for that, Mr. Clarkston. You let that fine meal settle awhile. Annie and I can see ourselves out," Michael said, reaching across the table and offering Richard his hand.

Richard shook Michael's hand and said, "It was wonderful meeting the two of you. We look forward to further associations with you and your families. Extend our greetings to your parents, won't you?"

Michael smiled, "Yes, sir. And thank you again."

"Walk me out, Brynn, please," Annie begged, linking her arm through Brynn's. Annie fairly dragged Brynn along chattering constantly. "Oh, your daddy's just a dream! Makes me wish I was still in school. And your mama! She's sooo pretty! And they're all so nice. Do you really think she'll mind if I come visit you again?"

"Of course not," Brynn assured her.

"Quit that gossipin' now, girls. It ain't polite," Michael said, stepping in front of the two young ladies and opening the front door.

Brynn avoided looking directly at Michael, for the warm sensation on her leg still burned from his earlier touch at the dinner table. Still, she could feel his eyes on her as she passed through the threshold with Annie.

"You all need a porch swing, Brynn," Annie commented as she noticed the lack of one on the Clarkston front porch. "Michael could build one for you, couldn't you, Michael?"

"Why sure. Porch swings are right necessary for certain...situations, you know, Miss Brynn," he chuckled.

Brynn looked up, her eyes widening as she saw him flirtatiously wink at her.

"That's right," Annie agreed. "Mama and Daddy sit out on ours every summer night sparkin' for hours!" Annie sighed heavily and continued on a different thought, "I guess we have to go. You have no idea, Brynn, how glad I am you've moved here. I can tell we're gonna be the best of friends. Can't you?"

"I agree," Brynn giggled. She was a bit startled when Annie embraced her quickly before skipping off.

"Hurry up, Michael! You want Mama to tan your hind end?" she called.

Michael chuckled. Brynn looked away as the penetrating blue of his eyes flickered mischievously at her. "Too bad the rain stopped earlier today, ain't it?"

Again, she looked at him with widened eyes, her mouth gaping open in astonishment at yet another insinuating remark.

"Careful, there, Miss Brynn. You might catch somethin' unexpected with that there baited trap of yours." Then he tipped his hat, smiled and turned, following his sister into the sunset.

"My goodness, Brynn!" Ophelia exclaimed as her daughter entered the kitchen and began helping to clear the table. "That boy must have every unmarried female heart in the west palpitating!"

"Yes. He's very handsome, isn't he?" Brynn remarked casually.

"That would be putting it mildly, I think," Ophelia smiled knowingly at her daughter.

"I would be more prone to say that he is far from being a boy," Richard interceded.

"You're a boy, too, Richard darling. 'Man' is just a general term, you know," Ophelia teased. "And he's so polite and well mannered. And that Annie! She's the very image of her mother. What a little chatter box. I think she's adorable."

"I wonder if she really meant it when she said I should come out and visit their farm," Brynn said quietly.

"I'm certain she did, dear," Richard encouraged.

Late that night, as Brynn lay in her bed attempting to go to sleep, her mind was awhirl with thoughts of the day, especially, the morning in Mrs. Johnson's backroom. She knew she would never forget the divine feel of Michael's skin against her palms, nor the heavenly scent of leather and bacon that was his. Each time she thought of those moments when he had asked her if she would slap him if he kissed her, her heart would swell to near bursting, and she wished to herself that she hadn't answered so properly. For if merely being near him sent her body and mind into fits of ecstatic delight, no doubt receiving a kiss from him would render her dead where she stood from such ecstasy.

When she finally drifted off to deep slumber, she dreamed of the moments in Mrs. Johnson's back room again and again and again.

CHAPTER THREE

"So they have this box lunch sale, you see. All the young women in town make a box lunch. Then the sheriff auctions each lunch off to the highest bidder. The man who wins the biddin' gets to have a nice little picnic with the girl of his choice. All the money collected goes to the school for deaf children over in Dove Creek. We all do it every year, honey...I hope you don't mind that I signed you up to make a lunch."

Brynn's mouth dropped open in astonishment when Mrs. Johnson mentioned it. "Mrs. Johnson! It sounds so...heathenistic! Men bidding on women!"

"They bid on the box lunch, sweetheart. It's all in fun and it's for a good cause. Shoot, if Mr.

Johnson hadn't bought my lunch so many years back in California…we might never have met and fallen in love," Mrs. Johnson chuckled.

"My mother won't approve I'm afraid," Brynn said.

"Oh, I already asked her about it when she was in this mornin'. She thought it was a sweet idea."

Brynn shook her head in disbelief. Her mother and father both had relaxed so much since their move west. Sometimes it astonished her how much more they enjoyed life.

"Hey there, Mrs. Johnson…you little vixen you," came Michael McCall's voice from the doorway.

Brynn turned to see him standing at the door handsomely grinning at her and Mrs. Johnson.

"Michael! How good to see you, boy. What are you in fer? I see your shirt ain't fallin' off ya today," Mrs. Johnson greeted him.

He walked to the counter. Folding his arms, he leaned casually on the counter next to Brynn. "I just come in to see if you had anythin'…interestin'," he said, smiling at Brynn. "Hey there, Miss Brynn. I ain't seen you in a week."

Brynn looked away, blushing. As warmth flooded her body, especially her rosy cheeks, she answered, "Yes. How have you been?"

"Oh, me? Just fine." Turning his attention to Mrs. Johnson, he said, "I come in for some supplies, sweetheart. I'm buildin' a porch swing for Brynn's mama and daddy."

Brynn's eyes widened as she looked at him in astonishment. "What?" she asked.

"I just come from your house, Miss Brynn. I told your daddy I'd be more'n happy to put up a swing out there on your front porch. I told him that if he wanted me to feel more comfortable when I was out on the front porch a-sparkin' with his daughter, he needed to get a swing up."

Mrs. Johnson snickered as Brynn screeched, "What? You didn't really? Did you?"

Michael chuckled sympathetically as he reached out and took her chin in his hand. "No, darlin'. Of course I didn't say that to your daddy. Now get that purty color back in your face."

Brynn sighed heavily with relief, but her breath was immediately taken away as Michael reached out and pulled her against him in a warm embrace. "I think I scared her, Mrs. Johnson," he muttered.

"You're a mean ol' tease, Michael McCall. Poor thing's as white as a sheet," Mrs. Johnson scolded.

Brynn's face had been smashed flat against Michael's massive and incredibly firm chest before he tipped her chin with one hand and looked down into her astonished and beautiful face. "I'm sorry, Miss Brynn. I was just teasin'. But I really am buildin' a swing for your mama. I asked her if'n she'd like one and she said yes," he explained.

"That's very kind of you," Brynn stammered as she gazed into his enchanting face.

"Well, Michael McCall! Whatever are you doing with that child?" Michael released Brynn abruptly at the sound of Annabelle Barrington's voice.

"If she ain't got the timin' of the devil," Mrs. Johnson muttered under her breath loud enough that Brynn still heard the comment.

"I scared her near clean out of her britches, Annabelle. Had to calm her down," Michael explained.

"Well, you have to be considerate of children. They take things completely to heart, Michael. Are you busy right now? Papa has a new pony! He's just brought it in from Denver and he wants you to take a look at it," Annabelle cooed, linking her arm through one of Michael's.

"Is it really a pony, Annabelle? Or is it a horse? I don't deal much in ponies," Michael said.

"It's a horse, silly. I meant to say that! I've just had a terrible time sleeping since I've returned from the east. It's too quiet here. Anyway, Daddy wants to know if you'll come and look the animal over."

"I'm pickin' up some things to build somethin' for Mrs. Clarkston. When I'm done here I'll run by for a minute 'fore I head home," Michael said.

"Can't you come right now, Michael?" Annabelle pleaded, batting her eyelashes.

"I'll be along shortly, Annabelle. Run on home and tell your daddy that for me," Michael repeated.

"Well, all right. But can't I just wait here with you instead? I have a few things to pick up myself."

"If'n you're wantin' to wait, go right ahead," Michael said, detaching her hand from his arm. "Here's a list of what I'm needin', Mrs. Johnson. You point it out and I'll get it. I don't want you luggin' this stuff over here for me."

"Whatever did he do to upset you so, Brynn?" Annabelle asked when Michael and Mrs. Johnson left the counter.

"He...he...was just teasing me. Nothing really," Brynn answered.

"Oh. Well, my Michael is a tease! He used to tease me something terrible when we were children. He even picked me up and dropped me in the creek at a town social when I was nine! I was so angry. But, of course, who can stay mad at him for long. I forgave him promptly. Were you in the store to buy something, or just to visit

Mrs. Johnson? I suppose you are painfully aware that Michael always comes in here to see her when he's in town. No doubt that's why you come to visit so often."

Brynn drew in a deep breath to calm herself and then said, "Actually, I've become quite attached to Mrs. Johnson. I just happened to be in here when Michael arrived. It's not as if I sit across the street and watch for him everyday and then just happen to show up any time he's here."

Annabelle's triumphant smile faded and her eyes narrowed. "You're a little young to be trying to catch his attention, Brynn."

"I don't have to try, Annabelle," Brynn retaliated. Then turning toward Mrs. Johnson and Michael she called, "I'll be off now, Mrs. Johnson. I feel the need for some fresh air and a brisk walk. Thank you for the visit. I guess I'll be seeing you at our house soon enough then, Mr. McCall?"

Michael's eyes twinkled knowingly and he said, "First minute I can get there, Miss Brynn."

"Good-bye, honey! You come on by tomorrow, you hear?" Mrs. Johnson called, waving at Brynn as she left the store.

"Have a nice day, Annabelle," Brynn called as she left the young woman standing in the store scowling angrily. She smiled to herself at her verbal victory over Annabelle. Then scolded herself in the next thought for dropping to the girl's own petty level.

———●———

Later that afternoon there was a knock on the front door.

"Brynn, dear...would you get that please? I'm up to my elbows in trying to find a way to bake a decent cake in this oven!" Ophelia sighed in irritation.

Brynn did, indeed, answer the knocking. The familiar thrill that filled her each time she found herself facing Michael McCall erupted once more as he greeted, "Hey there, Miss Brynn. I've come to take some measurements for our...the swing I'm buildin' for your family."

His smile was dazzling, and the toothpick between his teeth fluttered briefly.

"Is it that dashing young McCall boy I hear, Brynn?" Ophelia asked. She entered the parlor drying her hands on her apron. "Hello there, Michael. Have you come to start on the porch swing?"

"Yes, ma'am," he answered, tipping his hat. "I don't suppose you could spare your lovely daughter for a minute here. I need to measure some things out front."

Brynn shook her head, but her mother answered, "Well, of course, Michael. Whatever you need. You don't mind assisting him for a minute, do you, dear?"

Michael grinned slyly at Brynn and quickly winked. "Of course not, Mother," Brynn said. She was startled when Michael grabbed her hand and yanked her through the doorway the instant she agreed.

"I've got a cake or two to tend to," Ophelia called, as she turned and walked back toward the kitchen. "You just let me know if I can help, Michael. And mind my hollyhocks at the side of the porch! I'm proud as a princess about them."

"Yes, ma'am," he called.

"You're family's comin' to the barn raisin', right?" Michael asked as he handed Brynn one end of a tattered tape measure.

"Yes. We're planning on it. That's why Mother's trying to perfect her cakes," Brynn said with a smile.

"Hold that down there on the floor, like that," Michael said, pointing to the porch floor. "Well, it'll be fun. Lotta work for us men folk...but it's well worth it when the frame's up and we get to eatin' those goodies all the ladies bake. You want it to be at least two feet off the floor, you know," he said, stretching up his arm and placing the other end of the tape against the porch railing.

"Was Annabelle's father's horse a good one?" Brynn casually asked. She began to seeth at the thought of Michael spending time at Annabelle's home.

"It is purty good. I wasn't sure it would be. I thought maybe Annabelle was just blowin' smoke. She's always out for attention. But, it's a nice animal. He paid a purty price, too. I know the feller he bought it from 'cause he buys from me." Michael smiled and dropped his voice. "I'll let you in on a little secret, darlin'...I raised that stallion from a colt. I own his sire!"

Brynn smiled. "Why didn't he just buy it from you?"

"'Cause I sold him to the feller up in Denver. I guess he saw what good stock he was and decided to make himself a profit by sellin' him to Annabelle's daddy. Believe me, he did make a profit!"

"I think that's funny," Brynn giggled.

"Yeah. Me, too," Michael chuckled and dropped the tape measure. "What color are you wantin' this swing to be, Miss Brynn?"

"I don't know," she answered. "What would you suggest?"

"Won't matter none to me what color it is. I plan on sittin' on it in the dark anyhow," he answered and winked at her.

Brynn smiled and shook her head, all too pleased at his flirtation. "You are far too playful, Mr. McCall."

"What makes you think I'm always just teasin'?" he whispered with eyebrows raised questioningly.

"Because you...you..." she stammered.

"You just be sure you don't stand me up at that barn raisin' next week." Removing the toothpick from his mouth, he pricked her lip with it and placed it between her parted lips. "I got plans for you, little Miss Brynn Clarkston." Then he tipped his hat and said, "Tell your lovely mama that I'll have that swing up 'fore she knows it." He smiled at her and left.

Brynn watched him walk away fascinated by his movement. Little did she realize Michael meant his last remark literally. The next morning when her brother and sister bolted out the front door on their way to school, they called to Brynn and their mother to come outside. There, glistening white in the morning sun, was a perfect porch swing.

CHAPTER FOUR

It felt like a dream. Brynn rode in the back of the wagon with Sierra and Scottie. She pinched herself to make sure she was awake and not just dreaming. They were finally and actually on their way to Matthew and Mary McCall's farm. The day of the barn raising had seemed as if it would never arrive. Her father said they could attend when her mother had asked him about it. But, to actually be going was simply unbelievable.

Brynn smoothed the skirt of her new dress and pinched the sleeve heads to puff them. It had turned out nicely and Brynn's mother assured her endlessly that it was very becoming on her.

"That must be it there," Richard Clarkston said, pointing ahead of them. "Look at all the wagons! Must be every family and person in town here."

"My, yes!" Ophelia agreed. "What fun this will be!"

Brynn's stomach began to tie itself into square knots. The anticipation of seeing Michael McCall again was unnerving!

Brynn had not seen Michael since the day he came to measure the porch for the swing. She wondered if he would even remember the casual flirtations he bestowed upon her that day. Would he even be in attendance at the barn raising? After all, the barn to be raised today was his uncle's not his father's.

Unfortunately Brynn also had become better acquainted with Annabelle Barrington. This was not a positive experience, considering Annabelle saw herself as far too elite and beautiful to comfortably associate with the other girls in town, especially Brynn.

Whenever Annabelle spoke to Brynn, she wore a painful sneer on her face as though she had just tasted something unpleasant. Several times, Brynn discovered Annabelle studying her from across the street. Always, she wore a disgusted expression. Brynn had reconciled herself to the reality that Annabelle was simply a cliché snob. She tried to not take

Annabelle's expressions and condescending remarks too seriously.

As the wagon came to a halt near the other wagons Annabelle's shrill voice rang out, "Oh, I suppose it is necessary to attend these...these...little gatherings. Still, it's ever so dusty and dry out today. A girl's complexion might suffer dreadfully if she weren't skilled in protecting it."

Brynn caught sight of her standing nearby and talking to a tall, handsome young man who resembled Michael. As Richard assisted Ophelia from the wagon, Annabelle and the young man turned. Annabelle caught sight of Brynn. "Brynn! How delightful to see you! Haven't you a parasol, child?"

"No, I never bring one, Annabelle. I prefer to have a little natural color to my cheeks," Brynn answered, smiling sweetly.

"Touche, my dear," Ophelia mumbled, winking at Brynn.

Brynn felt triumphant and was thankful she had confided with her mother about Annabelle Barrington. She felt she had an ally—someone to support her should the other girl's subtle remarks start to penetrate her self-confidence.

"The Clarkstons?" the young man asked as he approached, his hand in greeting to Richard.

"Yes. And you are?" Richard inquired, taking the young man's hand and shaking it firmly.

"Matthew, Jr. I'm Matthew and Mary's oldest boy, sir. How glad I am to meet you."

Brynn felt the warmth gathering in her cheeks as the young man's gaze fell on her. A smile spread across his face as he said, "You must be Miss Brynn Clarkston."

"Yes, sir," she sputtered.

"I heard tell of you. My..." the young man looked up quickly to Brynn's parents and then continued, "My...uh...my mama told me that there was a right lovely young lady in the Clarkston family."

Brynn's blush at the compliment immediately turned to horror as Sierra popped up at her side and said, "I'm a Clarkston, too, you know."

Matthew squatted, tipped his hat back, and smiled at Sierra. "I can see that, Sweetie. And I'll tell ya a secret," he whispered. "My fancy runs to lovely young ladies with dark hair, big blue eyes and angel kisses sprinkled across their noses."

Sierra smiled and said, "They're freckles."

"Some folks calls 'em freckles, sugar, but I know they're little spots where the angels kiss people who are 'specially purty," he said, tweaking the girl's nose before standing again.

"I'm Annabelle Barrington, Mr. and Mrs. Clarkston," Annabelle interrupted, stepping between Matthew and Sierra. "I don't believe we've met yet."

"Oh, we've heard so much about you, dear," Ophelia said, with a smile.

"I'm certain you have. I've just returned from finishing school. And, as you know, that's a rarity in these small western towns," Annabelle informed them.

"My mama will be near to squealin' her head off when she finds out you've actually come, Mrs. Clarkston," Matthew said, taking Ophelia's arm and linking it with his own. "Do let me take you along to see her."

"Are all you McCall boys such gentlemen?" Ophelia asked.

"Every last one, ma'am. We get that from our daddies," he assured her.

"Come along, children. Let's go greet Mrs. McCall. Scottie. Scottie? Scottie has run off already!" Ophelia sighed, shaking her head.

"Boys will be boys, ma'am," Matthew commented. "He'll be fine. Can't get into much trouble around here."

"You don't know my Scottie," Ophelia reminded him.

"No. But I remember myself as a youngster, ma'am," he chuckled.

Brynn gave Annabelle an exaggerated smile as the family left her standing alone.

"Ophelia! Brynn!" Mary called as the Clarkston family approached the long table laden with every kind of baked good and food imaginable. "I'm so glad you've come! Did you have trouble finding us?"

"None at all, Mrs. McCall," Richard answered, placing Ophelia's perfectly baked and decorated cakes on the table.

"And I see you've met my Matthew." Mary smiled as she lovingly caressed her son's cheek. "Isn't he handsome, Ophelia?" she asked.

"Oh, my yes. And so polite and chivalrous," Ophelia agreed. "I have to admit the McCalls seem to have a very recognizable genetic heritage."

"Here's Matthew now," Mary said as a tall, attractive older version of Matthew, Jr. approached.

"I'm Matthew McCall. Mary has told me all about you," Matthew said, extending a hand to Richard.

"Richard Clarkston," Richard said as the two men shook hands.

"Here comes ol' Tom. Ain't he an ugly ol' cuss?" Matthew chuckled as another man approached.

Even though he was older, Brynn recognized this man from the picture in Mrs. Johnson 's back room. "Baker McCall," the man said, shaking Richard's hand firmly. "And I'm the best lookin' boy in the family. Matthew's just jealous," he chuckled, slapping his brother soundly on the back.

"Brynn! Brynn! Finally! I've been waitin' all mornin' for you to get here!" Annie squealed as she rushed forward. "Come on! There's all kinds of folks you need to meet." Annie dropped her voice to a whisper and added, "Ol' Beevis Bellmont even slicked back his hair for this occasion," she giggled.

Brynn smiled and looked to her mother who nodded, granting permission for her daughter to go off with Annie.

Once out of sight of the adults, Annie babbled endlessly. "Porter Jorgenson is here, Brynn! I can hardly contain myself! He's an absolute living dream! Wait 'til you see him...all tall like, and blond with the deepest brown eyes you ever saw! He's a bit older than me, though, and I don't think he knows I'm alive. But you wait—someday I'll get his attention. He's right over here! See him? That tall one. He's as tall as Michael, at least. Look. See him?"

Brynn looked in the direction Annie pointed and did, indeed, catch sight of a handsome young man fitting Annie's description. "Ain't he just a dream? I think I'm plum gone on him, Brynn. Dang it all anyway," Annie sighed.

"Believe me, Annie...I understand all too well," Brynn muttered, sighing heavily herself as she thought of Michael.

"But you're so pretty, Brynn! You catch everyone's attention! I'm so plain Jane and short. No one notices me." Annie sighed again. Brynn looked at her, her own mouth gaping open in disbelief at the girl's perception of herself.

"Baitin' flies again, Miss Brynn?" came Michael's whisper in Brynn's ear. Goose bumps broke over every inch of her body as his breath warmed her neck. Whirling around to meet him, she smiled at the sight of him in his clean white shirt and newer looking Levi's. She liked the way Levi's looked on Michael, and she secretly uttered a silent thank you to the man who had made them so appropriate for hard working men to wear.

"Mmmmmm mmmmm!" he exclaimed then, studying Brynn from head to toe. "Girl, you look good enough to eat."

Brynn's eyes widened at such a bold remark, but she managed a polite, "Thank you, Mr. McCall."

"What are you two little cats gawkin' at, Annie?" he asked, looking past them to the group of young men standing some ways off.

"That dreamy Porter Jorgenson. And you just keep your big trap shut, Michael McCall," Annie whispered.

"Who's lookin' at him? You or Miss Brynn here?" Michael asked, winking at Brynn.

"Me! Now quit teasin'," Annie scolded.

"Well, Mama sent me over to get you two. They're gettin' ready to start the barn. You gonna come on over and watch my muscles bulge whilst I'm workin', Miss Brynn?" Michael chuckled.

Brynn blushed to her heels and said calmly, "I'm interested to see how a barn raising comes off, yes."

He smiled and offered her his arm. Rather cautiously, Brynn laid her hand in the crook of it as he offered his other arm to his sister. "Well, come along then, girls. I'll tell you what, Annie," he said dropping his voice. "I'll see if I can talk ol' Porter into workin' without his shirt on. We wouldn't want him to get it dirty now, would we?"

Annie slugged her brother playfully in the shoulder. "Keep your mouth quiet, Michael. I got my own dirt on you as ammunition. Remember that." Michael chuckled.

———————●———————

The barn raising was, indeed, interesting and hard work. Brynn and her mother both gasped aloud in astonishment when, simultaneously, every man present with the last name McCall stripped his shirt off before beginning the work on the barn. Instead of gasping, Sierra simply muttered, "Wow!"

Brynn and Annie giggled as they watched Porter Jorgenson also strip his shirt after talking briefly with Michael. Michael turned around and winked at his little sister. Brynn smiled warmly. It was obvious the siblings shared a sweet relationship.

Brynn's eyes never once left Michael's muscular and capable form as he worked with the other men to raise the barn's massive frame. He was her own ideal of the perfect man. She reflected on the brief moments in Mrs. Johnson 's store when she had been embraced apologetically in his strong arms and against his firm, muscular torso.

A sigh escaped her lungs at the remembrance. Annie said, "Porter is so handsome, isn't he?"

Once the frame was successfully erected, the men attacked the food-laden table as if not one of them had eaten in a month. Annie pulled Brynn to one side and whispered, "You wanna see somethin' so romantic it'll send butterflies soarin' in your tummy?"

Brynn nodded and followed as her friend led the way to the house. As they approached, Brynn heard voices speaking in quiet intonations. Annie turned to Brynn. Putting an index finger to her lips, she indicated they be carefully silent. Brynn's eyes widened at the sight which met her eyes, as they peered around the corner of the house.

The beautiful and sophisticated Malaina McCall was standing with her back against the side of the house. An intense blush brazened her cheeks. Jackson McCall stood before her. A hand pressed firmly against the house on either side of Malaina's head. He was shirtless and leaning forward so that his forehead pressed against his wife's.

"Come on, darlin'...you still like me best this way, don't you now? No shirt and trappin' you up against a wall?" Jackson said in a low voice.

"You have absolutely no manners whatsoever, Jackson McCall," Malaina giggled.

"Maybe not, but it's all true, ain't it? Everything I promised you I would be when we got married. I still get your heart racin' when I catch you like this, now don't I?" he chuckled.

Malaina took his face between her lovely hands and nodded. "Yes you do, you monster. That's why I worry so about those boys of yours."

"Aw, they're just like their daddy, darlin'. No need to waste your time worryin' there."

Brynn watched, mesmerized as Annie's daddy then leaned forward capturing his wife's mouth in a deeply passionate kiss. Annie tugged at her sleeve, and Brynn followed her back to the others.

"Oh, my goodness! They are too wonderful!" Brynn exclaimed as they returned to the gathering.

Annie sighed heavily. "Yep. I ain't gonna get married 'til somebody makes me feel the way Daddy does Mama. Even to Porter Jorgenson."

Suddenly, Brynn was startled as a plate of blueberry pie was suddenly smashed against her.

"Oh, my! How carelessly clumsy of me," Annabelle gasped dramatically, having appeared from seemingly nowhere. "And blueberry of all things! Your dress is no doubt simply ruined!"

"You did that on purpose, Annabelle Barrington! You ol' biddy!" Annie snapped.

Brynn inhaled deeply as she wiped at the blueberries clinging to her bosom. "Fortunately it's an older dress, Annabelle. Don't concern yourself too much," Brynn said, forcing a forgiving smile. "I'll simply sponge it off a bit. It will just have to do for the rest of the evening." Leaving Annabelle looking quite vexed at not having provoked her, Brynn turned and left the others. As she walked away, she heard Annie still scolding Annabelle.

Once out of sight of the group of townspeople tears of anger, humiliation and disappointment began to escape her lovely blue eyes and trickle freely down her cheeks. How she detested that Annabelle Barrington! Every beautiful inch of her. She could only be thankful Michael had not been present to witness her humiliation at Annabelle's hands.

A watering trough stood near the old barn, and Brynn sighed heavily as she wiped tears from her cheeks.

"You're a better man than I would've been, Miss Brynn."

Brynn spun around and looked straight into the awe-inspiring face of Michael McCall.

"I'd a popped her square in the snout," he said, taking several steps toward her. His brow was puckered in a most unfamiliar frown as he looked at her and studied the large stain on her dress front.

"She would've triumphed then," Brynn responded, wiping at her tear stained cheeks once more. "It's what she wanted me to do."

"I know. And I would've jumped at the bait myself," Michael grumbled. "But, I suppose...bein' the lady you are...yer above such things, ain't ya?"

"Not really," Brynn said, looking away and trying to avoid his unsettling gaze. "I would've loved to have smashed the rest of that pie in her syrupy little face."

"Well," he chuckled, moving closer to her. "Next time you do just that, Miss Brynn."

Brynn cleared her throat nervously. Turning she walked to a nearby tree. "Maybe I will. At least I would've felt better about the ruination of this dress."

Taking a toothpick from his back pocket and placing it in his mouth, Michael followed her to the tree. "It's a right purty one, too. Ain't that the cloth you were pickin' out that first day I seen you in Mrs. Johnson's store?"

Brynn looked up at him, entirely flattered that he remembered. "Yes, it is," she answered. He smiled and she noticed the sound of the breeze through the leaves of the willow where they stood. She watched, entertained, as the tooth-pick in his mouth began to flutter up and down.

Reaching up, Michael took hold of a tree limb with both hands and leaned toward her a bit, letting the branch support some of his weight. "You know, Miss Brynn...blueberry is my favorite color."

Brynn smiled and said, "You're just trying to make me feel better."

"Oh, believe me, darlin'...I could make you feel better. And without saying one word."

Brynn blushed and shook her head in disbelief. "You're the worst tease I have ever met, Mr. McCall."

"I ain't teasin', Miss Brynn. It's the truth." His grin was mischievous as well as tantalizing.

"You know, I should slap you for even speaking of such things to me," she reminded him. She thought how utterly horrified her mother would be were she to overhear the conversation in which her daughter was involved.

He chuckled. As the musicians back at the gathering began to play, he let go of the tree limb and offered one hand to her. "May I have the pleasure, Miss Brynn?" he asked, bowing slightly as he looked into her face.

The bright smile left Brynn's face. Her hand went to her collar and she began anxiously toying with her cameo broach.

"I ain't the best dancer, but I can handle waltzin' all right," he added, motioning to her to take his hand.

Tentatively, she reached out and placed her small hand in his much larger one. The instant his fingers tightened around hers she knew she had made a grievous error. Every thread holding her being together was aware of his simple touch. As he pulled her closer to him and placed his other hand on her waist, she battled with every muscle in her body to keep from bolting from him.

"Yer other hand goes on my shoulder, darlin'," he reminded her. "You think I'm a mangy ol' flirt, don't ya?" he asked as he began to lead her in the waltz.

"What?" she asked, befuddled. The smell of leather and bacon filled her lungs as it had that day in Mrs. Johnson's back room. She could feel his breath in her hair and sensed the warmth from his body. Silently, she reached up and placed her hand lightly on his shoulder.

"You think I'm just teasin' you all the dern time. You probably think I tease every female in town the same way, now don't ya?"

She smiled without answering.

"Now, ain't this romantic? Us waltzin' under a willer...all secluded like? Nobody eyein' us but the breeze in the leaves and the stars?"

Startled by the sudden change in subject of conversation Brynn looked up at him.

"Just the right weather for sparkin', I say," he muttered, winking playfully.

"Oh, no, no, no," she whispered as he stopped waltzing. He dropped her hand and removed the toothpick from his mouth. "Oh, please no," she repeated, as he pulled her body flush with his own.

Brynn was certain he would be able to feel the feral hammering of her heart as it pounded within her chest. She could hear it in her own ears as it beat recklessly. She watched in silent awe as his head descended, and then she melted in his arms when his mouth touched her lips gently. She pulled away and averted her eyes shyly, but he took her chin and directed her gaze at him once more.

"I'm just gettin' yer feet wet, darlin'," he whispered. "Ain't nothin' to be afraid of where I'm concerned." He smiled at her and moistened his lips before bending to kiss her again.

His second kiss was more intense. Brynn feared that if he attempted to coax her further, she might submit to actually returning the kiss. As it was, every strand of her being fought valiantly to keep from succumbing to him.

"Brynn! Brynn?"

Brynn gasped and looked at Michael in horror. "My mother!" she whispered.

He smiled. "I guess she'll be findin' ya here in a minute, huh?" he said softly.

"Let me go!" Brynn pleaded as she struggled.

"Kiss me back, and I'll let you go, Miss Brynn," he chuckled.

"What! Are you insane? She's coming this way!"

"Brynn? Oh dear, Malaina. I hope she's not too upset," came Ophelia's voice on the breeze.

"Ain't that nice," Michael whispered smiling. "My mama's comin' on over, too."

Struggling Brynn pleaded, "Oh, please! Please, let me loose!"

"Kiss me first," he chuckled.

"Very well," she relented, and quickly kissed his rugged cheek before continuing with her struggles.

"No, no, no, darlin'! They're gettin' closer. You better fold." And his mouth was fierce and demanding on hers. This kiss was different from the previous playful ones. Brynn was tempted to return it. This kiss was conceived by an all powerful, provocative man obviously capable of rendering any female of the species willingly defenseless with one trifling touch. Though devastatingly brief, Michael's kiss exhausted the breath from Brynn's lungs. She stared at him in a daze as he gazed down at her.

"Now, you run along and put some dry stockin's on 'fore you catch cold, Miss Brynn," he whispered. Then pricking her lip lightly with his toothpick, he placed it between her parted lips before quickly leaving her alone under the willow tree.

Only moments had passed when Brynn, still in a daze found her mother and Michael's standing with her beneath the tree.

"There you are, sweetheart. Oh, I'm so sorry this had to happen," Ophelia comforted, truly understanding.

"Yes, Brynn. That Annabelle Barrington needs a good paddling if you ask me. But, Mary's youngest girl ran in and chose one of her dresses for you. You can change in the house and join us in a moment, okay?" Malaina said.

———•———

"There. Now that looks lovely!" Ophelia exclaimed as she studied her daughter.

"Yes! It fits perfectly. Now come on out and join us for the rest of the fun," Malaina said.

As Brynn and the two older women left the McCall house, Ophelia whispered to her daughter, "Sweetheart, I think you should spit that toothpick out before we return to the social."

At that moment, Brynn realized she indeed kept Michael's toothpick in her mouth the entire time she was changing her dress.

"Yes, Mother," she said and tucked the toothpick into the pocket of her dress.

"Oh dear, Ophelia," Malaina began, "I hope she hasn't picked up that nasty ol' habit from my boys! Why my Michael is forever and always chewin' on a..." Her words died away and one of her lovely eyebrows raised as she gave Brynn a lingering look.

Brynn blushed, and was puzzled when Malaina smiled happily.

———•———

"They're just starting another waltz," Ophelia said as they approached the large bonfire glowing near the food tables. "Brynn, just be a lady and ignore that haughty tapioca-faced girl."

"I'm fine, Mother. Really. You've no idea," Brynn said, as she returned Annie's friendly wave.

Annie dashed over to Brynn smiling radiantly. Brynn envied the girl for it was painfully apparent Annie would one day be Malaina's double.

"It fits perfect, don't it?" Annie squealed.

"Doesn't it," Malaina corrected.

"I'm so glad! Now you can come and dance and have fun!" Annie added, pulling Brynn toward a group of McCall relations.

"I'd a smacked her right in the kisser," Grant McCall stated as Brynn and Annie joined the group.

"Yeah, me too. She's such a stinker! I mean, it might be one thing if she were purty...but she ain't," another cousin added.

"Brynn's a lady. That's why she just walked away," Annie reminded.

"Next time I might be more inclined to conform to the general opinion," Brynn giggled.

"You get them feet all dried off, Miss Brynn?"

"Michael! Don't sneak up on Brynn like that! She nearly jumped out of her skin!" Annie scolded her brother as both she and Brynn turned to face him. Brynn blushed immediately upon seeing the knowing grin spread across his face.

"And for your information, it weren't her feet that got wet. It was her dress," Annie added.

"Don't you let Mama hear you talkin' so bad! She'll tan yer hide," Michael chuckled, still looking at Brynn. "I come to ask Miss Brynn for a dance. Miss Brynn?" he said, offering her his hand.

Instantly, Brynn's hand went to the cameo at her throat and she began to fidget.

"Oh, it's a waltz, Brynn! You have to!" Annie encouraged. "Where have you been anyway, Michael? Mama was lookin' all over for you."

"I...I had to change my shirt," he answered, still looking at Brynn knowingly. "You see, it's a long story...but there was this stain on..."

"I'd be honored, Mr. McCall," Brynn interrupted, abruptly taking his hand.

"You do ride by the seat of your britches, don't you?" he said, as they began the waltz.

"I thought you were going to say..." Brynn began.

"I was. Turns out, I got yer blueberry stain all over the front of my shirt. Now how do you think that happened? Not that I wanted to explain it to my mama, you understand."

Brynn cast uncertain eyes to the ground. "Why did you...under the tree before? You shouldn't tease people like that, you know."

"Yer just miffed 'cause I was right," he muttered.

"What do you mean?" she asked, looking up at him again.

"I was right—'bout bein' able to make you feel better."

Brynn rolled her eyes in exasperation. "You know what I mean. You shouldn't tease people like that."

"I don't tease people, Miss Brynn. Just you," he answered, Then added, "And I wasn't teasin' neither."

"You were," she whispered.

"I wasn't," he whispered back. Then bending so her ear could barely discern his breath from his words he added, "That there last kiss you let yourself have dern near knocked me on the seat of my pants, too."

"Quit teasing me!" Brynn whispered, smiling innocently at another couple dancing nearby who suspiciously glanced at her.

"You think I'm playin' with ya 'cause yer so young, don't you?" he said. His amused smile had been replaced by a frown.

Brynn guiltily dropped her eyes.

"Well, I got some information for you, Miss Brynn Clarkston," he said. "You ain't a baby girl no more. Better face up to that fact and prepare yerself for a grown-up man. Namely, me."

Brynn blankly stared at him, not believing what she had just heard. As her mind fought to comprehend the meaning of his words, the music ended, and he bowed to her quickly.

"Thank you, Miss Brynn. Now, if'n you'll excuse me...I gotta little matter to discuss with Miss Annabelle." And, before she could stall him, Michael McCall was across the way offering his hand to Annabelle Barrington.

"Oh, my goodness," Annie exclaimed as she came to stand next to Brynn. "I hope he don't make a scene! I bet he's steamin' mad about her ruinin' your dress, Brynn."

"Oh! You don't think he'll mention it to her, do you?" Brynn asked. She didn't want the situation to be any worse than it was.

"Oh, he won't mention it to her, as such. He'll make some smart aleck remark lettin' her know what a pain in the hind end she is. Then he'll walk away all smiles and muscles like nothin' happened. You watch. I know Michael like the back of my hand."

Brynn watched as Michael led Annabelle into a waltz. She was irritated at having to watch them dance. She did note that he didn't hold Annabelle as closely as he had held her.

Her stomach churned as she watched Annabelle sweetly smile up at Michael. Then, suddenly her smile faded, and she appeared to become indignant.

"See. Here he goes," Annie giggled.

Brynn saw Annabelle stiffen in Michael's embrace. Her eyes appeared to narrow as she looked up at him even though Michael grinned happily as he talked. As the music ended, Michael bowed slightly. Annabelle inhaled angrily, quickly turned and stomped away.

"She won't never smash pie on you again. I can promise you that, Brynn," Annie giggled.

"Miss Annie, would you pleasure me with a dance?" The unknown voice came from behind Brynn.

Brynn and Annie turned. Brynn was delighted to see Porter Jorgenson offering his hand to Annie.

"Me?" Annie asked, unsure he had actually spoken to her.

"Yes, ma'am," Porter said.

Nervously, Annie tucked a loose strand of hair behind her ear and placed her trembling hand in that of the young man's. "Thank you, Mr. Jorgenson. I would be honored," Annie said as she delightedly smiled up at him.

Brynn smiled with joy for her friend and watched them enter the group of waltzing couples. She stiffened, however, when Beevis Bellmont approached, kindly smiling at her.

"Miss Clarkston, would you do an ol' feller a favor and give me a dance?" he asked.

Brynn forced a smile. Placing her soft hand in his roughened, wrinkled one, she said, "My pleasure, Mr. Bellmont."

It was a dance to be bravely endured, but when it at last ended, Brynn was glad she had endured it, for the man seemed truly grateful.

"You're a kind soul, Miss Clarkston. Ain't many a young girl would go through a dance with me smilin' like you did. I thank you," the man said, tipping his hat.

"You're a very kind gentleman, sir," Brynn assured him, smiling sympathetically as Beevis left her with a bow.

———●———

The usual tingling sensation traveled through Brynn as she turned to face Michael. "Miss Brynn, I..." he began, stepping closer to her.

He was interrupted as a young man rode up on a horse and shouted, "They done robbed the bank in Dove Creek!"

"Robert! What you talkin' about, boy?" Michael said as the young man who resembled Michael dismounted his horse.

"I'm tellin' you, big brother, this robbery stuff is gettin' mighty close to home. I was comin' through Dove Creek this mornin' when I heard it. Them bandits done robbed the bank at Dove Creek! Shot the sheriff to boot! Dang! That's not more'n thirty-five, forty miles from here!"

"This here's my little brother, Miss Brynn. He's the adventurer of the family. Ain't home long enough to take a bath usually," Michael explained.

"Well, howdy do, Miss Brynn," the young man said with a smile. "I'm Robert McCall. Not quite as handsome as ol' Michael here. But I do fine, don't you think?"

Brynn giggled. "Yes, I can definitely see the similar characteristics."

"What you doin' ridin' in like a tornado, Robert?" Jackson McCall asked, approaching his sons.

"They done robbed the bank in Dove Creek, Daddy! Shot the sheriff, too," Robert answered.

"Well, I don't like the sound of that. That's too awful close to home," Jackson mumbled.

Baker and Matthew McCall soon joined the group and the discussion about the recent robbery. Brynn, feeling uncomfortable, slipped away and found her parents preparing to leave.

"We'll be in town next week for the box lunch sale, Brynn," Annie assured her friend. "Then, I'm gonna ask Mama when you can come out and spend some time with us on the farm! We'll have so much fun! You'll let her come, won't you, Mrs. Clarkston," Annie pleaded.

"If I have your mother's approval, then I suppose it would be all right," Ophelia agreed.

———•———

"What are you so deep in thought about, Brynn?" Richard asked his daughter as they drove home beneath the stars that warm summer's night.

"What, Daddy?" Brynn said, when she realized she had been addressed. Her thoughts were back under the willow tree where the ruggedly masculine, fantastically attractive Michael McCall had favored her with the most tantalizingly, tasty, passionate kiss she could ever have imagined.

CHAPTER FIVE

"Don't worry, Brynn dear," Annabelle Barrington whispered. "It can't possibly take the old goat more than an hour to eat his box lunch."

"What makes you so sure Mr. Bellmont won't bid on you?" Annie snapped in Brynn's defense.

Annabelle rolled her eyes and sighed in irritation. "Because there is a specific and very dashing young man who would never let my box lunch go to anyone but himself. And besides, I heard Beevis Bellmont tell Doctor Timmons that he intended to bid on Brynn's."

"Are ya'll ready?" Sheriff Barnes shouted. The crowd gathered in front of the general store and cheered. "Well, let's get on with the biddin' then!"

Annie McCall's box lunch was bid on first. Brynn was horrified when she realized the bidding was taking place with motions, nods, and indications from the crowd that made it impossible to tell who was bidding on what.

She watched as Annie bit her lip nervously. So far as Brynn could see, Porter Jorgenson did little more then run his fingers through his hair and fold his arms across his chest.

Several moments later, however, Sheriff Barnes chuckled, "Sold for two dollars, folks! Now, remember...ya'll wait 'til the bidding is completely finished 'fore ya run up to get yer lunch!"

Annie smiled proudly and poked Brynn in the ribs with her elbow. "Two whole dollars, Brynn! That beats anybody I can ever remember! And I think it was Porter who bid on my lunch!"

"Don't get your hopes up too high, Annie. He hardly moved," Brynn reminded her.

"I know! I was watchin'!" Annie squealed.

Brynn swallowed with great difficulty as her eyes fell to the kind yet homely face of Mr. Beevis Bellmont who sat grinning at her with adoration. Watch as she did, and like a hawk, Brynn could not tell who bid on and bought any of the other lunches. Then, it was Annabelle's turn. Brynn felt sick as she saw Michael appear seemingly from thin air, and prop himself against a hitching post across the street.

"Now we've got here Miss Annabelle Barrington and her box lunch. We all know what good cookin' Miss Annabelle turns out, don't we?" Sheriff Barnes shouted. "Who bids a quarter?"

Brynn watched intently, but Michael only took a toothpick from his pocket and placed it on his tongue.

"All right then...we've got twenty-five cents. Do I hear fifty?" Sheriff Barnes barked. "Fifty! A dollar. Do I hear a dollar?"

The bidding continued and Brynn looked at Annabelle when the price reached three dollars. The prim princess of plumage smiled mockingly at her.

"Sold! Three dollars! Boy doggy! What a price!" Sheriff Barnes chuckled as the crowd cheered. "Now, the final and pertiest box lunch goes with Miss Brynn Clarkston. Do I hear a dollar?"

Brynn watched in horror as Beevis Bellmont tipped his hat to the sheriff. She looked to her mother who nodded encouragingly in a show of strength and support.

"Good. Then do I hear a dollar fifty?" the sheriff barked. Brynn could discern no movement from anyone in the crowd, yet the sheriff continued, "Hold on, hold on, folks...I've just had a bid...yes, I read that as five dollars! Is that right, sir? Are you biddin' five dollars on Miss Clarkston's box?"

Brynn looked desperately at Mr. Bellmont who grinned triumphantly and nodded. She looked to Michael who stood still, the fluttering toothpick in his mouth the only thing that moved.

"Sold!" the sheriff shouted. And the crowd applauded wildly. "Five dollars! That's a town record, Miss Clarkston!" he congratulated. Brynn smiled, fighting to hold back tears of humiliation and disappointment pleading for release.

"Now, if you boys'll come on up here and pay yer money, you can be on yer way for a nice picnic lunch with a lovely companion. I remind you...behave yerselves, boys," the sheriff chuckled.

Brynn watched in horrified wonder as several men began to walk toward the general store's porch. Among them were Beevis Bellmont and Michael.

"It's only an hour, Brynn," Annabelle cooed as she rose in anticipation of her patron.

"Don't listen to her, Brynn," Annie whispered. "She's just mad 'cause you brought more'n she did. Michael wouldn't let Beevis Bellmont buy me or you."

Brynn smiled and tried to appear relieved. She watched as Michael stepped onto the porch and took a money bag from his pocket. Beevis Bellmont had already given Sheriff Barnes his money and was walking toward her. She forced a friendly smile as he approached but nearly burst into hysterical tears when Annabelle tapped the man on the shoulder, halting his advance and said, "She was hoping for someone else, Mr. Bellmont. But I'm sure you'll show her what a gentleman you can be."

Mr. Bellmont nodded and Brynn rose courageously to greet him. "You're ready to go then, Miss Barrington?" he asked Annabelle casually.

"I'm sorry, what?" Annabelle asked.

"I done bought yer lunch box, Miss Annabelle!" Beevis announced, taking Annabelle's hand and placing it in the crook of his arm. "Let's go have us a picnic!"

Annabelle looked back at Brynn who stood stunned, mouth gaping open. In that same moment, Michael pushed past Beevis saying, "Excuse me, Beeve. Gotta get over here to my lunch. I got me a terrible appetite this afternoon."

Then he was standing before her and Brynn looked up into his breathtaking face. "Close yer mouth, darlin'. You baitin' flies, or what?" Michael chuckled as he took the box lunch from her, holding it securely under one arm and taking her hand in his. "Annie," he whispered aside to his sister. "Ol' Porter oughta be comin' up any minute to claim you. You can relax."

Annie squealed with delight and began looking for Porter frantically. She giggled as she watched him pay the sheriff and approach her, tipping his hat.

"You? You bought me...my lunch?" Brynn asked Michael in a stunned whisper.

"Who did you think bought it, Miss Brynn?"

"But I was watching you. You never moved!"

"I told ya before, darlin'...a toothpick is a mighty handy habit. Sheriff Barnes knows me well enough, too." He fluttered the toothpick in his mouth and laughed as he led her toward his wagon. "Yer face dern near drained of life when ol' Beevis started headin' on over."

Brynn smiled. She could smile because she was so greatly relieved and elated at the same moment. "I suppose he's a very nice man. I really shouldn't have reacted that way."

"Are you joshin'?" Michael asked. "He smells like mothballs and mice nests! Yer lucky you got me instead."

"Yes. I know," Brynn admitted.

"'Sides...I'm better lookin', ain't I?"

"More conceited, I'd say."

"No. It's just...well, I got an old hound at home that's better lookin' than ol' Beeve," Michael whispered.

Brynn smiled to herself. What a beautiful day it had turned out to be. She felt mildly self-conscious as people stared as they walked to the wagon. Michael tipped his hat and smiled, muttering a pleasant, "How ya doin'," to each of the onlookers as they passed. At last they reached his wagon and Brynn found herself being lifted effortlessly off her feet and into the wagon.

"Comfy?" Michael asked, as he looked up at her and grinned. Then he climbed up. Sitting next to her on the buckboard, he took the reins in hand snapping them gently. "I know this perfect picnic spot, Miss Brynn. Don't you worry, you're in real capable hands," he assured her. "This spot's got a crick, a nice patch of blue-grass and a big ol' weepin' willer tree to boot."

Brynn quickly looked to him. His words reminded her of her past experience with this Michael McCall and a willow tree.

He winked slyly and added, "Gives off a lot of coolin' shade, you see." Brynn glanced away, blushing excessively. "What ya got in the box there for lunch?"

Brynn cleared her throat and looked at him once again. "Fried chicken," she stated.

"My favorite," Michael chuckled. "Anything else? I got me a mighty big appetite today. You're gonna have to satisfy it somehow."

Brynn began to wonder how much longer she could endure his implicating remarks and still remain unruffled. "Potato salad, fresh rolls, and chocolate cake," she answered.

"Mmmm. Sounds tasty. So," he said, changing the direction of their conversation as they traveled. "You're gettin' to be purty good friends with my sister, ain't ya?"

"Annie? Yes, I think she's fabulous! She's so very beautiful. She looks just like your mother," Brynn remarked.

"Yeah, she's a cutie. My mama is purty near to gorgeous, ain't she? You should see her and Daddy's weddin' picture! I tell you, they was quite the attractive couple."

"I'm certain of that!"

"Well, you just be sure you don't go listenin' to any of that hound slobber Annie goes around tellin' about me. I ain't half as bad as she makes out," Michael chuckled.

"She's only got good things to say about you," Brynn assured him. "You seem to get along so well together. I'm still too easily irritated by my siblings."

"We're older, Annie and me, that's all. You'll see...that little imp of a brother of yours will grow up to be one of your best friends. And that darlin' little sister, her name's Sierra, right? She's a sweetheart. I think she's plum gone on my cousin Matthew."

"This week," Brynn giggled.

"Oh, she's a fickle pickle, is she?" Michael chuckled. "I hope you ain't inherited that characteristic, too!"

"No, no, no. Not me!" Brynn sighed, thinking of her sister's endless interest in romance. "I just have that one vision of..." She stopped herself from confessing her deepest thoughts to him. She had almost told him that ever since she was a small girl like Sierra, she had sheltered an ideal image of the man she wanted to spend her life with. She had almost confessed this secret to the very mortal envisionment of that ideal.

"Of what?" he prodded.

"Of...of..." she stammered.

"Of..." he prodded again.

"Of...of what a man should be," she finished awkwardly.

"Oh," he chuckled. "You mean you just have that one vision of me tucked away, huh?"

Horrified at his hitting the proverbial nail on the head, Brynn's mouth dropped open and she stared at him in silence.

"I'm just joshin' with ya, Miss Brynn," he laughed. "No need to go baitin' bugs again."

Brynn immediately clamped her mouth shut and drew in an unsettled breath.

"Here ya go," he announced, reining the team to a halt. "Purty, ain't it?"

Brynn nodded as she surveyed the lovely area to which he had driven them. It was even lovelier than she had envisioned. He jumped from the wagon and motioned her to follow.

"Come on, darlin'. I'm starvin'," he said, as she placed her hand tentatively in his. "Watch this," he instructed. He knelt down on one knee, making a step for her with his other thigh. "Purty impressive, huh? Learned this one from my daddy."

"Oh, I can't possibly..." Brynn began. He tugged on her hand and she involuntarily stepped down with one foot which landed squarely on his thigh as he had intended. He took her other hand as she stepped down again and helped her steady herself when her feet finally met the ground. Then standing, he reached up and removed the box lunch from its place on the buckboard.

"Hold on here a minute," he said and reaching into the wagon, he produced a plaid blanket. "See, I thought ahead."

Brynn raised her eyebrows and smiled as he took her arm directing her forward.

———●———

They enjoyed the lunch Brynn had prepared and all the while Michael made flattering comments about her culinary skills. After they finished eating, Michael leaned back against the enormous willow tree. His legs stretched out long and straight in front of him, and he contentedly took a toothpick from his pocket and began chewing it.

"Now that was worth five dollars," he sighed, smiling at her.

Brynn tucked her legs under her skirt and said, "No meal is worth five dollars, Mr. McCall. But I'm sure the deaf children in the home will appreciate your generosity."

"Weren't nothin' generous about it, Miss Brynn. I just wanted to get you out here alone under a willer tree again." He winked at her teasingly as he pulled his hat down over his eyes.

"I wonder if Annie is enjoying her picnic," Brynn muttered, looking around her at the beautiful landscape.

"Oh, yes. I'm sure she is. I lent ol' Porter Jorgenson the two dollars to buy her with. I knew she'd a died if he hadn't been able to take her," Michael mumbled.

Brynn looked at him in pleasant surprise. "That is so sweet, Mr. McCall. She had her heart set on going with him."

"I know. I'm a sucker for my sister."

Brynn shook her head and marveled at his sentiment. He was too good to be real. No man possessed all the positive qualities this one seemed to. She began to wonder what secret flaws were hidden within him. She must have sighed out loud at the thought because he quickly lifted his hat from his eyes.

"Gettin' tired of me already, huh?" he asked.

"Oh, no! Of course not!" she exclaimed.

"Well, let's go for a stroll. Ya wanna?" He stood up and replacing his hat in its proper position, he reached for her hand.

"Very well," Brynn agreed, rising to her feet.

"There's an interesting little rock formation in the crick down here a ways. Come on, you'll like it," he said, pulling her along.

"This is such a lovely area," Brynn sighed as they followed the creek's downward babbling.

"Yep. Now, look here," he instructed, crouching down and peering into the water. "See that?"

Brynn knelt and bending over the edge of the creek's bank, she peering into the clear water. She was startled and gasped when she saw her own reflection looking back at her—not the faint reflection from the water's surface, but an obvious mirrored reflection made by something that lay beneath.

"See. It's a real thick sheet of mica. Works just like a mirror. Ain't that kinda interestin'?" he asked.

"Oh, yes! I've never seen such a large piece before," she agreed.

Michael sat down on his seat and looked around. "This here's one of my favorite places. Just up stream aways is where Daddy did ol' Black Wolf in."

Brynn looked at him quickly. "This close to town?"

"Yep. Me and Robert used to play in that ol' cave all the time. We ain't had no Indian trouble since I was a baby. Government packed 'em all off to the reservations." He stood up and drew in a deep breath. "I suppose I better be gettin' you on back to town. Don't want yer daddy comin' after me with a rifle, now do we?"

"I suppose," Brynn mumbled as every ounce of joy exited her body. It had been a dream come true, picnicking with Michael McCall in seclusion. It was over now and he would go home to his way of life. She looked up as she felt him take her hand and her breathing quickened as she beheld the serious expression on his face.

"I made sure I drug you off far enough that yer mama won't be callin' for you this time," he whispered as a mischievous grin spread across his face.

"You're right. We better be getting back," Brynn said, wrenching her hand free and walking briskly toward the tree.

Having returned to the empty box lunch and picnic blanket that still lay in the grass beneath the willow, she turned to face him as he said, "I'm sorry, Miss Brynn. I guess I shouldn't press you like that."

Brynn leaned back against the tree trunk and sighed heavily. "It's just that I know you're only teasing me. You shouldn't play with people's feelings like that, Michael." Realizing that his first name rather than 'Mr. McCall' had slipped from her lips, she looked up to find him staring intently at her. He moved closer to her, removing the toothpick from his mouth and flicking it away. She realized she was trapped between the tree trunk and the gorgeous speciman of masculinity.

"Now, I like that. You just mighta got away this time..." he mumbled as he bent toward her, "if you hadn't a called me Michael, Brynn." He bent toward her until his mouth was a breath away from her own. "I suppose you'd slap me if'n I tried to steal a kiss, right?"

"No," she breathed.

"Wouldn't matter either way, Brynn," he whispered.

His kiss was like warm cider on a winter's day. As his lips pressed firmly against her own, Brynn felt the blissful warmth of the kiss fill her body. She sensed his hand on her face and realized he cupped her chin in it, pulling her toward him as if it were possible for her face to be closer. His voice saying her name echoed through her mind as her senses thrilled to his touch.

"You gonna slap me, Brynn?" he whispered, interrupting their shared interaction.

"No," she managed to mouth, though no sound escaped her lips.

Her chin still held gently in his hand, he tipped her head to one side and she jumped as his mouth placed a moist caress on her neck just below her ear. Reflexively, her hands gripped his forearm as goose bumps broke over her body like a tumultuous tidal wave. He released her chin, and taking her hands in his own, he laced his fingers with hers. Then he pulled her body to his, holding their hands at her back as his mouth fiercely commanded hers to return the unrestrained ardor it incited.

His kiss was powerful, yet still bridled, and when he released her hands and let his arms fully embrace her, she instinctively allowed her hands to wander caressively over his broad shoulders. Brynn had never imagined that being held and kissed in such a manner would be such blissful delight. She knew she was experiencing true and unequaled ecstasy at the hand of Michael McCall. His breathing was quickened and strained as his mouth guided hers in the impassioned exchange. He ended their bandying with softer, less threatening kisses, finally sighing heavily as he released her and straightened, clearing his throat.

"I better get you headed home," he said, mumbling something under his breath about having to talk with her daddy if they didn't leave then.

———————•———————

As they traveled back toward town, Michael asked, "You plannin' on bein' some big singer like your mama when you grow up?"

Brynn looked at him quickly, irritated by his inference that she was still a child. It vexed her so much that he would even intimate it that she snapped back a little more defensively than she meant to, "No. My ambitions go more toward gaining a firm education. Women aren't as accepted as they should be in the universities and I plan to be the exception."

"You mean, you plan on having a profession of your own?"

"Yes. Someday."

He became oddly quiet and Brynn wondered if she had angered him by her snappy remark.

"And you?" she asked finally, attempting to rekindle the conversation.

"Me?" he mumbled. "I'm just a poor farm boy, remember?" he spat sharply. "I ain't got no ambition 'cept livin' a long life full of hard work and fun, Miss Clarkston."

"I didn't mean to imply that..." she began.

"Ah, I know, I know. I fly off the handle too all quick. You just go on and be whatever you want, Brynn. An opera singer, university professor or rich man's wife. It's your life to live, now ain't it?" he muttered.

"I don't want any of those things," Brynn exclaimed. A sense of panic was beginning to rise within her and she didn't know why.

"You deserve those things. A girl like you...well, you ain't meant for these parts and the harshness that sometimes goes along with it. I don't know what your daddy was thinkin' movin' you all out here."

"He was thinking quite clearly and I've only just now come to realize it," Brynn muttered. A thousand thoughts were flying about in her mind then. She remembered the noise and chaos of the city. The smell of burning tobacco, coal, garbage, stale liquor. She remembered the worry and fatigue always evident on her father's face when he returned very late each evening from the university. She noted the bronze and healthy pink that colored Sierra's and Scottie's faces now that they were able to play outside in the fresh air. She thought of her mother's lovely voice echoing through the house as it hummed or sang a tune almost constantly. Her mother's singing had been absent in their city home on a daily basis. She thought of the immaculately dressed young men that would come to call. Always clean and tidy they were, hair slicked flat on their heads, collars so high their ears could perch on the rim of them. She looked over to the indescribably handsome man that held a set of reins and sat next to her. His hair blew back slightly in the breeze, his Levi's were clean, yet worn, especially, she had noticed, in the seat. She blushed and scolded herself inwardly for noticing such things as the seat of Michael McCall's Levi's.

"Thank you for purchasing my box lunch, Michael," she said so softly it was nearly a whisper. "I don't know why you choose to be so kind and to...flirt with me so, but I do want to thank you."

"Thank you, Brynn. It was a mighty fine meal," he said bluntly.

"I've done something, haven't I?" she asked. She sensed the change in him and it frightened her. The teasing, friendly manner she had come to know was gone. In its place was aggravation and distance.

"You ain't done nothin'," he sighed heavily. "Nothin' at all. And I apologize for my behavior back at the crick. It won't happen again."

Brynn felt tears sizzling at the brink of her eyes and she stated angrily, "Please stop this wagon."

So commandingly did she order it that Michael immediately reined the team to an abrupt halt.

"I knew it," she cried as she fought to withhold the hot moisture gathering profusely in her lovely blue eyes. "I knew you were just a...just a...philanderer! I suppose you do this to every new girl that moves into town! Don't you? Just take her heart firmly in hand and squeeze it to death!"

"Philanderer?" he repeated.

"Yes! Philanderer!" she squealed as she quickly hopped down from the wagon and began marching toward town.

"That's a nasty name, Brynn," he called after her as he too jumped down from the wagon. "I don't take to name callin'! Especially when it's me bein' called it!"

"And to think!" she shouted, stopping and turning to face him. "To think I let you...surrendered my...let you...actually force yourself on me back there! What a chuckle you must have had at my expense."

"Wait a minute!" Michael growled, taking hold of her arm. "You know that ain't it at all, Brynn. I ain't like that. You know that. It's just that now I realize you got other things in mind than I do."

"I don't. I only said those things because you spoke down to me so!" The tears ran down her cheeks at last as she was no longer able to contain them.

"Oh geez, don't cry, Brynn. I ain't got no backbone when it comes to women crying," he whined, frowning defeatedly.

"I'm not crying. And I am grown up. Whether old men like you think so or not," she said, yanking her arm free and marching forward once again. She gasped as she was suddenly caught in his arms as he pulled her back against his body. "Let me go!" she ordered, struggling in his embrace.

"I know you're grown up, Brynn. And...I believe it's time I started treatin' you that way, ain't it?" he whispered and her body nearly melted as his mouth placed a moist, persistent kiss on her neck just below her ear. "You see," he whispered, brushing her hair aside and placing another kiss at the back of her neck. "I wasn't sure...you are young, whether or not you want to admit it, darlin'. Young enough that these sorts of situations might make you bolt and run. I have to watch my step. You understand that, don't you?"

"I understand that you're using me for your own amusement! You must think I'm terribly naive!" she sniffled.

Michael turned Brynn to face him. "I know I say a lot of teasin' things, Brynn. It's my way.

But I ain't funnin' when I kiss you. That's just the man in me bein' a bit impatient I guess." He brushed a strand of hair from her face and wiped a tear from her cheek with his thumb. "There's somethin' about you, Brynn Clarkston. Somethin' that gets ol' Michael McCall completely wrapped around your little finger." He kissed her forehead tenderly. "Don't you see? You could get me to do anything you wanted just by lookin' at me with them beautiful eyes of yours. First chance I get, I'm comin' over to talk to your daddy about you. We gotta get that new porch swing broke in, don't we?"

"You're teasing me," Brynn said.

Michael chuckled and pulled Brynn against him tightly. "I'm not! Dang, you're a humble little thing, you know that?"

"Do you mean it, Michael? You're not just mocking me because you know I..." Brynn stammered.

"Because I know what?" he prodded.

"Because you know," she repeated.

"Because I know that when I'm not around you think about me all the time? Because I know that sometimes when you're alone you wish I was holdin' you like I am now? Because I know that when I kiss you, you wish it never had to end?" he whispered as he tipped her tear streaked face up to meet his own handsome one. Brynn's mouth dropped open slightly in awe at his words fitting her feelings for him so perfectly. Michael chuckled at the perplexed expression on her face. "You're wonderin' how I could know all that, ain't you?" His thumb traced her parted lips tenderly. "I know, 'cause they're the same things I think about you, Miss Brynn Clarkston." Then, as his thumb continued to caress her lips he whispered, "Now let's put that fly trap to use. You done caught somethin' this time, darlin'." And his mouth met hers in a moist and deeply sincere kiss. She was satisfied then with a sure knowledge that he was, indeed, honest in his feelings for her. His kiss was strong and commanding, yet filled with integrity. Brynn knew then that by some blessed divine stroke of fate, she had managed to capture the attention of the impeccably, both physically and inwardly, developed Michael McCall.

CHAPTER SIX

The next morning, Brynn awoke with the euphoric knowledge that Michael found her interesting. Yes, attractive even. Any other young woman, say Annabelle Barrington for instance, would no doubt become slightly puffed up in her own vanity faced with such a wonderful revelation. Yet Brynn, blessed with boundless humility, still found herself doubtful that she had even experienced the previous afternoon's events in the company of Michael.

Sitting erect in her bed suddenly, she muttered to herself, "Maybe I simply dreamed it all!"

"Brynn! Quickly! Get up!" came Sierra's excited voice from the hallway. "The bank has been robbed, Brynn! Our very own bank! Right here in town!"

Brynn dressed quickly. When she heard a knocking on the door she rushed out to see who would be visiting.

"Oh, Ophelia!" Malaina McCall cried as she entered the Clarkston house. "Michael's missing! We can't find him! We haven't seen him since last evening at dinner and that monster, Sheriff Barnes, has the audacity to imply that he may have been involved in the bank robbery late last night!"

"What?" Brynn gasped.

"Has he been here, Brynn darling?" Malaina asked frantically. "I thought he might be here!"

"No," Brynn answered, horribly anxious about Michael's well being.

"He was here, somewhat late last night, Malaina," Ophelia informed her friend. "He spoke to Richard about..."

"Yes, yes. I know. He spoke with us about it beforehand. Do you know where he went after that?" Malaina asked, dabbing at a tear on her cheek.

"No, I don't," Ophelia admitted as she began wringing her apron nervously.

"Whatever shall we do?" Malaina cried. "He's my baby! I'm so worried. He wouldn't do this unless something was terribly wrong! Perhaps he's been hurt somehow."

———•———

As the day wore on the sheriff and his deputy, Clyde Tate, searched the countryside for the men who had robbed the bank. And, they looked for Michael McCall.

"Why was he here last night, Daddy?" Brynn asked her father as they sat together at the kitchen table that afternoon.

"I think you know why, young lady. At least, I assume that you would. Otherwise, I would judge you to be very naive indeed," Richard said, smiling at his daughter.

"What did he say?" Brynn asked, trying to appear casually curious.

"I think I'll let you hear it from him, sweetheart. He'll be back soon enough." And he was, in a mere few minutes.

"Michael!" Brynn exclaimed upon opening the door and finding him standing before her. "Michael! Your family is worried sick! Where have you..."

"I need to see your daddy right away, Brynn. Quickly," he interrupted, pushing his way into the house and closing the door behind him.

Brynn immediately noticed the profuse perspiration trickling down his temples. Furthermore, his clothes were dirty and his frown was frighteningly serious. "All right," she said.

She returned several moments later with her father who immediately started questioning Michael.

"Where have you been, Michael? Sheriff Barnes suspects you of taking the bank," Richard Clarkston stated.

"I'm sure he's lookin' for someone to pin it on, sir. He done it himself," Michael growled.

"What?" Brynn asked in disbelief.

"He done it, Mr. Clarkston. I seen him. I seen Sheriff Barnes and Clyde Tate comin' out of the bank late last night. That's why he's lookin' for me. He shot me, so he's probably wonderin' if I'm still breathin'," Michael explained bluntly.

"Where are you hit, Michael?" Richard asked, concern in his voice.

"Oh, it ain't hardly nothin', sir," Michael mumbled. But Brynn gasped again as her father took Michael by the shoulders and turned him around, revealing the back of his shirt soaked with blood originating at his left shoulder.

"I need you to run out to my daddy's place and tell him to ride over to Telluride and get some law that ain't gone bad," Michael explained. "I'm sure Barnes is watchin' my family like a hawk, and I can't go there. Also, I'm in need of some bandages...maybe some soap? Then I'll be on my way."

"You're not going anywhere, Michael!" Richard ordered. "Brynn and Mrs. Clarkston need to clean that wound out! Of course I'll let your family know you're well...but I'll go for help. It would be less suspicious."

"I can't let you do that, Mr. Clarkston. This ain't your trouble," Michael stated.

"If the law officers in this town are crooked...it's everyone's trouble, young man."

"Daddy, Mother won't be home for a while. She's gone down with Sierra and Scottie to check on Mrs. Johnson ," Brynn stammered. Michael was incredibly pale and appeared to be dangerously fatigued. "But I can do this. You need to leave now. There's no time to stand around."

"True. I'll be off then." Taking the young man's hand in his own, Richard Clarkston shook it firmly. "I knew something like this was about. You're too good a man to be involved in thievery."

"I hope I'm not bringin' any danger down on your family, Mr. Clarkston," Michael muttered.

"I'd have hung you myself if you hadn't come to me," Richard assured him. "Clean him up good, Brynn. That bullet's been in there far too long. It didn't come out the other side, did it, Michael?"

Michael shook his head, frowning. "It's in there all right. I can feel it just under the skin of the front side here."

"Dig it out, Brynn," her father instructed as he took his hat from the hook behind the door. "You must remove it! Do you understand?"

Brynn nodded obediently as she stared with terrified anxiety at the battered man before her.

"Be quick, Brynn. Then hide him well. They might suspect he'd come here for help." Brynn watched as her father closed the door behind him without another word. She wanted to cry out to him, to stop him from leaving her with such a terrifying burden as tending to the wound. Instead, she took Michael's hand in her own and turned toward the kitchen.

"I can feel it, there...just under the skin, Brynn," he said. "I can't figure why it didn't just shoot on out. Hurts like the dickens, though."

"Sit down here," Brynn ordered as she pulled a chair away from the kitchen table. In silence, she went to the cupboard where her mother stored the medical supplies. Taking things that she guessed she would need, she laid them on the table and lit the fire in the oven to warm the water in the kettle.

"Remove your shirt please, Michael," she commanded.

"Yeah, you like me best half neked, don't ya?" he teased. The grimace on his face made it obvious that he was in great pain as he struggled with the shirt.

Picking up a pair of scissors that she had laid out, Brynn took hold of his collar and began cutting the shirt straight down the back. "It's ruined anyway, right? What's the point of causing you unnecessary discomfort?" she muttered to herself as she removed the bloody fabric from his body. She gasped when she saw the wound. It was completely caked with dried blood. "Oh, Michael," she whispered as she felt tears brimming in her eyes.

"Go at it from the front, Brynn. Like your daddy said, just cut me where I show you, and you'll find it easy," he mumbled.

It was only at that moment that she realized what both her father and Michael were instructing. She must cut into his flesh, scar his beautiful body, if she was going to even attempt to extract the bullet! Sitting down in a chair across from him she said, "I...I can't. I can't possibly..."

"You have to, darlin'," he growled, taking hold of her arm firmly. "I can't do it myself. I'm too tired and weak. Listen to me...if I pass out..."

"What?" she exclaimed in alarm. "You can't! I need you to..."

"If I pass out," he began again, squeezing her arm firmly, "just dig that little cuss outta there. Wash the wound good with hot soap and water...back and front. Soap up your finger real good and clean it inside...as deep as you can go, darlin'. Now, don't lose yer head on me, Brynn. You want me to live long enough to corner you under that ol' willer outside of town again, don't ya?"

Brynn began shaking her head slowly as the tears leaped from her eyes and ran down her cheeks. "I...I..."

Reaching down, Michael pulled a large knife from his boot and offered it to her. "Here. Is that water hot yet? Dunk this in there, then I'll show you where to cut me."

Brushing the tears from her cheeks, Brynn did as Michael instructed. Sitting in a chair across from him once more, she said, "Very well."

"I'm gonna lay myself on the floor, darlin'. Might flinch too hard otherwise. You sit on my belly and..." he began.

"I can't possibly!" she shrieked.

Again he took hold of her arm firmly. "Brynn, ain't nobody else in this house, right?"

"No. They're all gone."

"Then somebody has to help hold me down just in case I turn out to be a pansy while you're cuttin'," he explained.

"You've never in your life been a pansy," she said.

"Ain't never had a bullet cut outta me in my life neither," he answered as he stretched out on Mrs. Clarkston's immaculate kitchen floor.

With great reservation, Brynn sat across his stomach and stared anxiously at the area of his chest he indicated.

"See there, it's bruisin'. Just cut like this," he instructed, motioning horizontally across the area. "You ready? Can't feel much worse than gettin' shot in the first place, right?" he said, attempting to chuckle lightly.

"I can't! I can't cause you such pain!" Brynn cried.

"Darlin'...ain't nothin' could hurt more'n it already does."

"Well, shouldn't I get you something to bite on?" Brynn asked. "A stick? Maybe a wooden spoon would do."

"Darlin', if'n I can keep my wits about me when you're this close, then I can certainly hold still while you're diggin' a bullet outta my body. 'Cause if there's one thing I've mastered since you moved into town, it's self control." He attempted to chuckle at his own teasing. Then, taking the hem of her skirt and wrapping his right hand in it tightly, he said, "Okay now. Let's get it over with." Then he closed his fantastic blue eyes and waited.

Taking the knife firmly in her unsteady hand, Brynn quickly cut the area. Michael flinched slightly. Without opening his eyes he said, "You're gonna have to do more'n scratch it, Brynn."

She felt his grip tighten on her skirt and her own tears spilled freely onto his chest as she tried once more, pushing the tip of the knife deeper into the fresh wound she had made. His body tensed fiercely beneath her own weight as she did so and he grunted slightly. Brynn was nearly undone as she watched the bright red blood begin to trickle down onto the kitchen floor.

"It may be hard to get a hold on. You may have to make that cut bigger," he muttered in a voice that revealed an endurance of great pain.

"I'll get it," she whispered and pressed the wound with her thumb, trying to feel the threatening bullet. "I feel it!" she exclaimed.

"Then dig it out, girl! It hurts like..." he mumbled.

With intense trepidation, Brynn inserted her index finger into the wound. Immediately she felt the hardness of metal.

"Come on, Brynn! It's gonna take more'n one finger!" he shouted as his body stiffened.

Quickly, she stuck her thumb into the wound as well. Oh! What a terrible feeling it was to be probing around in his wounded flesh with the knowledge that she was causing him such intense pain. Then she felt the metal between her thumb and finger and yanked it hard, successfully extracting it from his wound. It slipped from her fingers wet with his blood and made a clicking sound as it skipped across the floor, leaving a trail of bloody red dots.

Michael sighed heavily and his grip on the fabric of her skirt loosened. "Now clean it out quick! It hurts like..." he mumbled.

Quickly, Brynn did as he had previously instructed. Once she had washed and rinsed both wounds, she bandaged them and helped him to sit against the wall. His breathing was labored as if he'd just run a great distance, perspiration still hung in heavy beads on his face and forehead.

"I think I just need a glass of water and I'll be fine, darlin'," he mumbled. His eyes closed again as Brynn rushed to the pump at the sink. Returning hastily, she held the glass to his lips as he drank. At some point, she tipped the glass too much and the water spilled over his chest.

"I'm sorry," she apologized, wiping at water with her hand.

"Feels good. Ain't had me a tub since day 'fore yesterday," he whispered.

Brynn knew he was tired. Retrieving a pillow from the sofa in the parlor, she helped him to lie down on the kitchen floor, too afraid to move him any more than that motion alone required.

As his breathing steadied and slowed, Brynn knew he was resting, though fitfully. Going to the pump, she wet a cloth, wringing it out before using it to bathe his face, arms and chest. When she had finished, she glanced about her noting the mess her mother's kitchen was in. The thought went through her mind that her mother would be nothing less than livid when she saw the chaos and blood, but propping herself up against the wall next to Michael, she closed her eyes for a moment. Removing the bullet and cleaning the wounds had taken every bit of strength from her.

———•———

"Wow! What a mess! Look at all that blood!"

Brynn's eyes fluttered open to behold her mother and Sierra standing over her, their mouths gaping open in astonishment. Scottie was running around the room investigating Michael's blood stained shirt, blood stained knife, and the horrendous pool of blood that had begun to dry on the floor where Brynn had first laid Michael to work on him.

"Brynn!" Ophelia Clarkston whispered, in awe at the sight that lay before her. "Is he...is he..."

"Is he dead?" Scottie finished for her, squatting down next to Michael and studying his face curiously.

"No," Brynn answered. Then jumping to her feet, she spilled out the story Michael had told her father, explaining where he had gone.

Ophelia inhaled determinedly and said, "You've got to take him out of here. Sheriff Barnes was asking me only ten minutes ago if you had seen Michael today. He said he'd like to come by and talk with you. Quickly, Brynn! Wake him! You must get him away from here," her mother ordered. Ophelia, being the courageous, cool-headed woman she was, saw the danger and knew the solution. "Sierra, quickly...clean up this mess! Scottie, take that shirt out and drop it down the hole in the outhouse! Hurry! Brynn, get him out of here!"

"I'm sorry, Mrs. Clarkston," Michael said, pulling himself to a sitting position. "I shouldn't have come here."

"Don't be ridiculous, Michael! Of course you should've come here! We know just what to do, don't we, Brynn?" Brynn nodded. "Don't come home until you're certain he's all right."

"I don't want her helpin' me any longer, Mrs. Clarkston. It's too dangerous. I'll be fine on my own," Michael grumbled, retrieving his blood-ied knife from the floor and returning it to its place in his boot. As he stood and tried to walk forward, he stumbled, barely catching himself on the table before falling.

"Quickly, Brynn. Get him away from here," Ophelia ordered. "They'll surely find him."

Brynn took Michael's right arm and placed it around her shoulders. "Come along, Michael. Hurry!"

"Hurry, she says," he muttered as he stumbled toward the back door. "Just get me to where I'll be all right, then I want you to get right home."

————•————

Evening was descending by the time Brynn got Michael to the cave. She was thankful the weather was warm. She knew she would never find her way home in the dark even if she had harbored any intention of leaving Michael while injured or in danger, which she didn't.

"It's near the crick, darlin'. I'll be needin' water. Now you get home," Michael mumbled. His speech was slurred and unsteady. Brynn helped him to sit down inside the cave against a wall.

"I'm not leaving, Michael. And you are in no condition to fight me about that fact," Brynn whispered, as she placed her hand on his forehead which was uncomfortably warm.

"You got me there, darlin'," he admitted. "'Sides, I always wanted to spend some time alone with you in a dark cave." In the next moment, his breathing slowed and Brynn knew he was at long last resting.

He would sleep deeply for some time, she was sure. Taking advantage of her time alone with him, she ran one hand caressively over his pale face. "I love you, Michael McCall," she whispered. He was so hurt, and so handsome, and so wonderful that tears filled her eyes once more at the thought of his having such considerate feelings toward her.

———•———

The rattle woke her instantly, for even though her own ears had never actually heard the sound before, she knew instinctively what originated it.

"Michael?" she whispered. But there came no reply and Brynn sensed he was not in the cave. Sitting up slowly, she turned and saw the snake coiled just behind her. Its hideous tongue flickered as its tail stood erect rattling. She knew it would strike and she turned her back to it immediately, screaming when she felt the snake's fangs sink into the back of her left shoulder.

"Brynn?" came Michael's voice from just outside the cave's mouth. "Brynn!" he said again as he realized what had happened. Brynn watched still stunned as Michael stepped firmly on the snake's head, pulled the knife from his boot and sliced the reptile's head off swiftly. Then, spitting on the knife and wiping it on his pants, he shoved Brynn forward onto her stomach and sat himself soundly on her legs.

"Hold still," he ordered in a growl as he ripped the fabric of her dress exposing the wound. Brynn bit her lip as she felt him cut her shoulder where the serpent's deadly fangs had pierced her body. Michael sucked on the wound brutally, spitting the blood from his mouth and then repeating the process until Brynn could feel a numbing sensation replacing the pain of the bite. Quickly turning her over onto her back, he said emphatically, "It was a small snake, darlin'. You'll be fine. You might get sick, but you ain't done in. Do you understand me?"

Brynn nodded and brushed the tears from her cheeks. Sitting up, she looked at the body of the snake which lay near its decapitated head, still twitching now and again. Michael sat down against the cave wall, his eyes closing for a moment as his head fell forward.

"I shouldn't have left you here alone. I'm sorry," he apologized.

The shoulder where she had been bitten was painful and throbbing, yet Brynn could only think of the pallid lack of color on Michael's face.

"Are you all right, Michael?" she asked, moving toward him.

"No!" he shouted, looking up angrily. "I shoulda never come to your house! This here's all my fault! I shoulda tried to get home! I thought I was gonna drop dead of a heart attack when I come back in here and saw that danged snake had bit you! It took ten years offa my life, girl! I still ain't breathin' regular." He wiped the perspiration from his forehead with one hand.

"I meant, how's your shoulder? Are you feeling better than you did last evening?" Brynn asked, deeply touched at the effect her injury had on him.

"Oh, that. It's fine. It's sore and I feel weak...but I'm fine. You feelin' sick yet?" he asked.

"No," Brynn answered honestly.

"Well, I musta sucked a pint a blood outta you. Maybe you won't get sick. At least, I hope you're well enough that I don't have to carry you home. I'm not sure I'm up to that just yet."

"I'm not going anywhere until it's safe for you to go home," Brynn informed him as she studied the torn fabric hanging open and exposing her shoulder.

"You're goin' home right here in a minute, Brynn. This ain't your problem and I was wrong to drag your family into this. I didn't know what else to do, 'cause we can't let Barnes and Tate get away with this. I'm sure they're the ones that's been doin' all the robbin' in this area. I hope your daddy can get back soon. But, I'm gettin' you home right now," he added, standing up again. He swayed slightly. Brynn rose, taking hold of his arm to help support him.

"You're staying right here and I am, too, Michael McCall," she ordered. "You've lost a lot of blood, not to mention enduring the constant pain. Sit down here and rest."

"I promised your mama, Brynn," he mumbled as his hands went to his head. He swayed again and Brynn was able to push him into a sitting position.

"My mother knows what kind of shape you're in. And it's no shape to be moving around," Brynn told him.

"You better check them wounds and make sure there ain't no infection startin'," he mumbled, closing his eyes as his head fell back against the cave wall.

Carefully, Brynn removed the bandages she had placed on his shoulder the night before. Fresh ones were needed but the wounds, hideous as they were, looked clean and were beginning to heal.

"I meant the ones on your own shoulder, darlin'," Michael chuckled.

"Oh," Brynn said.

Michael stood up slowly and pulled Brynn to her feet. "You still got that bar of soap that you used on me in your apron pocket?" he asked, extending his hand toward her.

"Um...yes," she said, withdrawing the soap from its place in her apron and placing it in his hand. "But, I have to finish your bandages."

"First things first, Brynn. I didn't clean that knife too good 'fore I used it on you." Taking her hand, he led her from the cave and toward the stream. "It's gonna sting you realize," he said as he wet the bar of soap in the water and rubbed it between his hands making a thick lather. Brynn nodded, and he began washing the wound. "Your daddy would shoot me in the kneecaps if he seen me rubbin' your bare skin like this," he muttered to himself as his hands and fingers worked to clean the wound. "But then again, I'm sure he wouldn't want no infection startin' in it."

Brynn winced at the stinging pain the process caused, but at his touch, even in this specific circumstance, she asked her questioning thoughts out loud. "What were you doing at my home the night you were shot?"

"I was talkin' to your daddy," he answered plainly.

"About what?"

"About you."

"What about me?" she asked as her hopes began to soar.

"I done told you I was gonna have me a talk with him, Brynn. Didn't you take me serious?" Michael chuckled.

"What did you talk to him about? I mean...regarding me?" she asked, wincing as he scrubbed at her wound with the palm of his hand.

"I done told him the truth! What else? I told him that you were a brazen woman who tried to corrupt me under that ol' willer outside o' town."

Brynn gasped, turning to face him, her mouth dropping open in horrified astonishment at his remark. Michael laughed, entertained by her expression.

"Oh, darlin'," he chuckled, taking her in his arms and pulling her against his warm body. "I'm only teasin' you. Of course I didn't tell your daddy that. Even though it's the truth."

"It is not," Brynn defended herself, letting herself be held tightly in his embrace.

"I'm sorry, Brynn. I'm sorry I've put you in danger. I never would've dragged you into this if I'd been in my right mind," he said as he stroked her hair gently.

"There's nowhere on earth I'd rather be, Michael," Brynn confessed in an inaudible whisper.

"What's that?" he asked.

"I said...I'm the one who dragged you out here," she answered.

"I owe you my life," he whispered.

"I owe you mine," she whispered, looking up into his handsome face which wore an expression of tender appreciation.

Sighing heavily, Michael kissed her forehead gently. "Let's get this rinsed off," he said, releasing her and squatting down next to the creek. Filling his hands with water, he refreshed himself by drinking the cool liquid. Then he pulled Brynn down next to him and rinsed her wound, patting it dry with the torn fabric of her dress. Brynn's flesh tingled as Michael placed a light kiss on her bare shoulder.

"I can't spend another night in that cave with you, Brynn," he whispered as his mouth caressed her neck teasingly. "Believe me...I have to get you home."

"Do you think badly of me because I'm not trying to..."

"'Cause you're not trying to get away from me?" he asked, turning her face toward his. Brynn nodded. "I'm glad you're not trying to get away, darlin'. I ain't got as much strength as usual to hang on to you." This time Brynn didn't struggle when his mouth found hers.

Instead, she returned his kiss thoroughly, rejoicing in the power and passion he radiated. His skin was smooth and warm and soft beneath her hands. He sat down promptly on the ground, pulling her onto his lap and cradling her in his arms as his mouth worked an enchanting spell of ecstatic passion with its skillful kisses.

Suddenly, Brynn felt the first horrid wrenching feeling in her stomach. Pulling away from Michael quickly, she doubled over as a sickening nausea engulfed her.

"Come on, darlin'," Michael said, helping her to her feet. "Let's get back to shelter and have you lay down."

"I'm fine, really," Brynn assured him as large beads of perspiration appeared across her forehead.

"Sorry little cuss," Michael muttered, glaring at the decapitated snake as he helped Brynn to sit down against the cave's inner wall. "I think we oughta eat it for breakfast."

Brynn clamped her hand over her mouth to help stop the heaving in her stomach at the thought of eating a snake. Michael put a hand to Brynn's forehead and said, "Come dark, I'm goin' back to town to fetch your mama and see if your daddy's back yet. I don't want to be draggin' you all over, though. Here, lay down," he instructed her.

"What are you doing?" Brynn cried, startled when she felt Michael tugging at the hem of her petticoats.

As Brynn's petticoats slipped down from her waist and over her feet Michael said, "Well, darlin', you need somethin' soft for your head. And unless you're wantin' to have a purty quick lesson in anatomy...I best not be takin' anything else of mine off." Wadding up the garment, he tucked it gently under her head. "I'm thinkin' maybe you're just hungry and that's addin' to your feelin' so poorly. I'll go out and dig you somethin' up to munch on."

"Oh, no! Stay here!" Brynn pleaded as fear gripped her.

"I'll be right back. There's some wild strawberries growin' not far off. Rest your little head, darlin'." And he left.

CHAPTER SEVEN

"So," Brynn said as she ate the last strawberry Michael had gathered earlier in the day. "What did you talk to my daddy about?"

Michael was fatigued and his injuries were dealing him great pain. Brynn could see he was in need of sleep. Yet, he would not rest. He had been correct about her need for nourishment and after having eaten the delicious sun-warmed berries, she felt quite recovered. He worried her. He was perspiring profusely again, and once more the color had left his face.

"Oh, horses, bridles, nails. Things the like," he mumbled as his eyes closed for a moment. "Did I ever tell you that my mama and daddy spent a night together in this cave 'fore they was married?" he asked changing the subject, eyes still closed.

"No. Tell me," Brynn prodded, scooting up next to him. As she watched the sun already starting to set, she wondered why Michael was so evasive about revealing the particulars of his conversation with her father. She sighed, delighted by the brilliant pinks and purples that colored the sky like a freshly rendered oil painting.

Michael cleared his throat, eyes still closed. "You remember the ol' Indian that daddy did in, right?"

"Mmmm hmmm," Brynn answered.

"There was a big blizzard goin' on and Daddy couldn't get Mama home. She was in danger of freezin' to death so he brung her in here to warm her up." He chuckled then and his eyes opened as he turned toward Brynn. "Can you imagine how irate my mama musta been when my daddy forced her to put on a pair of men's red flannels?"

Brynn smiled and put a hand to his brow to wipe the beads of perspiration away. "What happened?"

"Daddy won a nickel," he said, his voice dropping. His words were muddled. "I can't keep my eyes open, Brynn," he mumbled as his beautiful blue eyes closed once again.

"Don't try. You need rest," Brynn whispered as his breathing slowed and he fell asleep at long last. Folding her petticoats neatly, she pushed him gently. He unconsciously leaned over as she helped his massive form to lay flat on the ground, his head positioned on the petticoat pillow.

They couldn't build a fire. No doubt the light would be seen by anyone riding near. Until Brynn's father was able to return with honest lawmen, it wasn't safe to reveal their location. Fortunately, it was a warm summer night and a fire wasn't needed. But, as the sun set completely and the moonlight did not penetrate very far into the cave, the wilderness noises and darkness began to unsettle Brynn. She had been far too fatigued the night before to be bothered. Tonight was different. As the wound in her shoulder throbbed and she sat next to the seriously injured and weakened man she adored, her strange surroundings frightened her.

Suddenly, she jumped, startled by the sound of an owl hooting somewhere just outside the cave. She was startled again as something warm touched her hand.

"It's just the night sounds, darlin'," Michael whispered and his hand caressively traveled up her arm. "If you listen, you'll find a kind of strange security in them." She sensed he was pulling himself to a sitting position as he added, "Hear the crick? Don't that sound soothin'?" He tugged at her arm and she moved closer. "Hear that? That's a little ol' barn owl."

As Michael pulled Brynn against his warm body, she melted to him, completely comforted and knowing she was safe in his arms. "Please be well," she whispered to him.

"I'm fine, Brynn. Just needed a few extra winks," he assured her. "Listen. You can hear Uncle Tom's new calf bawlin'. We ain't far from his farm, you know."

Brynn could hear something that was strange to her ears. It bothered her at first with its sad sound until she heard a low call that was similar.

"See? His mama found him fast," Michael whispered. "How's that shoulder?" he asked as his hand traveled gently over the sore area on Brynn's back.

"It's in much better shape than yours is," Brynn reminded him.

"I'm goin' then," he said. "You'll be fine here, Brynn." He made an effort to stand.

"Oh! No!" she pleaded, clinging tightly to his arm. "Don't leave me! I'll go with you!"

"I don't want you with me if I run into trouble, Brynn," he told her firmly. He stood and walked toward the cave's entrance.

"Please, Michael!" she cried, going after him. As he stepped out of the cave the moonlight shone brightly on his tall, handsome form.

He smiled down at her and said, "I'm feelin' purty perky now, darlin'. And—well, I think it's best if we both get home as soon as we can."

"Well, of course, but..." she began.

"I told you before, Brynn," he said firmly, brushing her cheek with the back of his hand. "I can't spend another night here with you. It's too...too...I need to get you home or else your daddy's gonna change his mind."

"About what?" she asked with a sinking feeling.

"If they catch me, they won't get you. So, if I ain't back by sun up...you start on home by yourself. Just follow the crick down. It goes right past town." He turned to walk away.

"Michael?" she called, reaching out and taking hold of his arm. "Hurry, please! I'm not very brave."

He reached out and took her quickly in his embrace. "Now that there's a lie if I ever heard one." He took her throat in one powerful hand, caressing her jaw with his thumb. Then without delay his delicious kiss was hers once more. His arms tightened around her like a vise and his impassioned, demanding mouth seemed unable to quench his desire for her response. Interrupting their affections, he took her chin in hand and said, "Do you understand why we have to get back, Brynn?"

"Yes. To find out if my father's back so you can be free from danger," she answered.

"No," he stated firmly. He bent kissing her again with such intensity that his unshaven face scratched her own soft one. His mouth moved to her neck kissing it briefly before finding the bareness of her exposed shoulder. "I'm a strong man, Brynn. But even the strongest men have their weaknesses. You're mine. Do you understand?"

"Yes," she answered, at last admitting to herself that his implication did, indeed, point in her direction.

He turned and left abruptly. When she could no longer see him in the dark of the night, Brynn returned to the cave and waited.

———●———

"Well, looky, looky. I believe we got the bait, Sheriff."

Brynn opened her eyes and gasped as she looked up to see Clyde Tate staring down at her, a mocking smile branded across his face.

"We figured you woulda helped the boy out, Miss Clarkston," Sheriff Barnes chuckled. "But where's he run off to?"

"He's gone," Brynn stated. "He went to..."

"He left you here all by your lonesome, Miss Clarkston?" Sheriff Barnes asked as he reached out, pulled her roughly to her feet and tugged at her torn dress. Brynn slapped his hand, then his face. He only continued to chuckle. "He'll be back, I've no doubt. Ol' Michael McCall wouldn't leave you here alone too long. He's too much of a gentleman for that. Besides, I bet he's wantin' to get his money's worth where you're concerned anyway."

"Oh, that's right. That ol' boy paid...what was it? Ten dollars for you, girl?" Clyde Tate asked, smiling wickedly.

"I think it were fifteen total," Sheriff Barnes answered.

"What are you talking about?" Brynn snapped.

"At the box lunch the other day. Michael gave ol' Beevis ten dollars to buy Miss Annabelle. Then he paid five for you. That's fifteen I reckon."

"He's not coming back," Brynn said. "He's gone to some town up north to find some honest law officers."

Brynn winced and put her hand to the cheek that Sheriff Barnes slapped at that moment. "He'll be back. He's got his hat tipped for you, girl. What? You think the whole town is blind?"

"More'n likely. None of us saw through your yeller hide," Michael said from behind.

Both men spun around to see Michael McCall facing them from the cave's opening.

"Michael!" Brynn cried. She was terrified now that he had been found by Sheriff Barnes and Tate. And he was alone!

"Leave her be, Barnes. You ain't got no fight with her," Michael said, frowning at the two men with disgust.

"No. But we do with you. And I know if it weren't for the fact that this little filly is in our company, you'd put up a fight. You McCalls think you can lick anybody," Sheriff Barnes said.

"That's 'cause we can," Michael growled.

"Maybe. That's why we're glad we found your little petunie here first. You ain't gonna give us no trouble if she's in the middle, now are you?" Sheriff Barnes caressed Brynn's exposed shoulder.

"You touch her again, Barnes...and you're dead where you stand," Michael threatened.

Barnes and Tate both began laughing. "Look at you, McCall. You look like something the cat dragged in! You ain't in no shape to be a threatenin' us," Tate chuckled.

Brynn's mind was whirling. She knew they were right. Michael was battered and weakened. He couldn't possibly take them both on and triumph. She would be their tool to destroy him. But, she was wrong. Michael lunged forward suddenly, kicking Barnes squarely in the stomach and laying Tate out on the cave floor with one swift blow of his powerful fist. Instantly, Brynn dashed through the mouth of the cave, having seen the opportunity to escape provided by Michael.

"Come on! Annie's gone for help!" Michael shouted. He took her hand and began running around to the other side of the rock formation that had housed them. Brynn heard the gunshot and saw Michael flinch, but he still pulled her with him. "Here! Get down!" he told her, shoving her behind a large boulder. Leaving with his back against the rock he said, "I've gotta get you out of here!"

Brynn gazed in horror at the blood she saw coming from a fresh wound in Michael's side. "Michael! You've been..." she began.

"It's only a graze. Let's go!" Taking her hand, he pulled her into an opening in between the rocks. A tree grew near the opening and

Brynn could discern at once that it would hide the crevice perfectly. Pulling her tightly against him, Michael said, "Shhh."

In the next moment, Barnes and Tate appeared and looked around carefully. "Where'd they go to?" Barnes growled. "There ain't nowhere to go!"

"It's that danged McCall blood. They's slipperier than snakes," Tate mumbled.

Brynn clung tightly to Michael. They would kill him if they found him. She knew that. They were ruthless criminals. Reaching down toward his boot, Michael drew the knife from a sheath hidden there. He looked at Brynn intently and mouthed, "Stay here." She shook her head adamantly and clung tighter to him. "Stay here!" his lips repeated. He broke free of her. Jumping from behind the tree, he drove the knife into Barnes' rib cage.

"You'll die like a dog!" Tate shouted and fired. Michael fell backward, another fresh flesh wound vivid across his right forearm. Tate chuckled triumphantly as he leveled his gun at the fallen hero. "You cocky pile of..."

His words were silenced as Michael threw his knife. It flew swiftly through the air, striking Tate squarely in the chest. The man stumbled forward, then fell to the ground motionless.

Michael collapsed where he lay and Brynn rushed to him, falling to her knees at his side.

"Brynn!" Richard Clarkston called.

"Daddy! Quickly! He's been hurt again. Hurry!" Brynn cried as she cradled Michael's head in her lap.

Richard Clarkston, Jackson McCall, and two strangers wearing badges dismounted their horses. "Let's get him into town to the doctor," Jackson said, as Richard helped him lift his son onto a horse. Jackson's expression plainly showed his worry and concern for his son. His face had paled immediately upon seeing Michael's condition. Brynn wiped her tears on her soiled sleeve as Jackson's strong hands stroked Michael's hair. "Hang on there, son," he said. "Your daddy's come for ya now."

Barnes, still alive, raised his head and pointing his gun at Michael's limp form said, "That boy's under arrest."

Brynn watched as the brutally handsome father of the brutally handsome son walked to where the sheriff lay. "You dirty, yeller dog," Jackson mumbled just before his powerful fist met the man's jaw, rendering him unconscious once more.

CHAPTER EIGHT

"Wow! Look at all the bloody cuts and stuff!" Scottie exclaimed. Michael began rebuttoning his shirt after showing the boy his wounds. They were still very gruesome to look at, even two days after the doctor finally had been able to tend to them.

"You're so brave, Mr. McCall," Sierra sighed, gazing at him in wonderment.

"I was so glad when Michael found me and we knew the two of you were all right!" Annie exclaimed to Brynn. "I was just on my way to town to talk to your mother, Brynn, when I saw him, and I was so scared when he sent me for help. I thought sure Sheriff Barnes would know I was up to somethin' when he stopped me on my way into town!" Annie put her hand to her chest as she reminisced about the frightening moments.

"It wasn't smart thinkin' when I had Brynn take me to that cave in the first place," Michael said, standing and stretching his stiff limbs. "I shoulda known Barnes would've thought of that cave sooner or later—given its history concernin' our family and all."

Brynn nodded. "It's because he came to talk to Daddy that night. If he had stayed home...if...this never would've happened," Brynn mumbled.

"That ain't true at all, Brynn," Annie argued.

"Brynn?" Michael said. "Can I see you out-side for a minute?"

———●———

"What's that I heard you sayin' to Annie?" he asked once they were outside the Clarks-ton house.

"It's true. If you had stayed home that night..." she began.

"If I'd a stayed home that night...I never woulda got to spend them nights alone with you," he chuckled pulling her down so she sat next to him on the porch swing.

"It's not funny, Michael! What was so im-portant that you had to come out that late to see my daddy?" she cried as tears traveled slowly down her cheeks.

"You're serious, ain't you?" he asked, brushing the tears from her cheeks. "You're shakin' my confidence here a bit, darlin'."

"How am I shaking your confidence?" Brynn lacked vanity. And, she was still afraid to believe that this fabulously handsome and older man sitting next to her could feel anything beyond friendship toward her. She was completely sincere in her question.

"What do you think I came to see your daddy about that night, Brynn?" he asked.

Brynn dropped her eyes to the ground, but spoke the truth even though she faced certain humiliation. "I...I...I was in hopes that you came to ask...to ask if you could...court me," she managed to sputter.

Michael broke into amused laughter. Humiliated, Brynn stood and began to walk away from him.

Catching her arm, he said, "Darlin', you've got to be the most humble woman on this earth!"

"What do you mean by that?" she asked sharply.

Michael drew Brynn into his arms and she struggled, angry with him for laughing at her. But when he quickly flicked the ever present toothpick from his lips and his delicious mouth coaxed hers into a tantalizing kiss, she ceased in her effort to flee.

"Don't you know, darlin'?" he whispered, as he held her hand to his lips and kissed it tenderly. "I...I couldn't tell you before, during that time we was held up in the cave. I wasn't sure...well, I wasn't sure I'd be around to..." He chuckled and kissed her hand once more. "I asked your daddy if I could marry you."

"What?" Brynn asked, her mouth gaping open in disbelief.

"I knew that first time I saw you in Mrs. Johnson's store that I wanted you. Just you. You're perfect for me. I love you, Brynn Clarkston." Brynn looked away shyly. "You're not thinkin' of breakin' my heart, now are you?" he asked.

"Me? Break your heart?" Brynn asked.

"I gotta have you, Brynn. Your heart, your mind, your body. It all has to be mine. I can see my baby girls and boys in those blue eyes of yours. And, if'n you don't say you'll marry me...well, I know a certain cave that is perfect for convincin' you," Michael whispered, smiling as he caused the swing to sway back and forth.

"I do love you," Brynn whispered, allowing her hands to caress his unshaven face. "I've always loved you. Did my daddy agree?" she asked, suddenly fearful her father had refused.

"He said I had to ask you," Michael whispered as his lips brushed her cheek.

"Then ask me," Brynn whispered, as his kiss tickled her neck. It was true! She knew, at last that it was true! Marvelously and blessedly true!

"Will you marry me, Brynn?" His voice was deep, quiet and impassioned.

Brynn felt her heart swell with the exhilaration of a dream come to life. "Yes," she whispered. "You know I will."

"You're in for it now, darlin'. You realize of course...I been holding back my best kisses," he said, as he teasingly kissed the corner of her mouth.

"That's impossible," she giggled. Then, Michael McCall proved to Brynn that he had, indeed, been holding back the best.

Other Books From Marcia Lynn McClure

The Heavenly Surrender
Visions of Ransom Lake
Shackles of Honor
Dusty Britches
The Fragrance of Her Name
Desert Fire

*Coming Soon

An Old Fashioned Romance

Read a preview
of the
Forthcoming

An Old Fashioned
Romance

**The Saga
Continues
with**

*An Old Fashioned
Romance*

**by
Marcia Lynn McClure**

Excerpt from
An Old Fashioned Romance

As she sat studying and appreciating her good friends, Breck was too preoccupied to perceive the hush that fell over the patrons at Marcelli's in that moment. In fact, it wasn't until she noticed her friends all looking at her, smiles stretching from ear to ear, that she realized something was afoot.

"What?" she asked, glancing down at her beautiful pumpkin sweater. Had she spilled sauce on it, she wondered.

Suddenly, she gasped as a black-gloved hand covered her mouth from behind. Next a man's voice, his breath hot on her neck, whispered in her ear, "Be still. The Highwayman of Tanglewood owns you now."

Breck recognized the phrase as one of her favorites from the book she so adored. However, she did not recognize the voice. The man's hand still covered her mouth tightly, but Breck could see the delight blazing across her friends' faces. *'So this was what they were up to all week,'* she thought. They had hired someone to be her Highwayman of Tanglewood.

Breck tried to push the man's hand from her mouth so she could turn and see him. But he tightened his grip, coaxing her to rise from her seat as he whispered, "Do not struggle. I'll not harm you. I simply intend to have you." Whoever was playing the Highwayman was delivering his lines straight from the book and with perfection. As she stood, Breck began to giggle for the expressions on her friends' faces were worth a lifetime of other expressions from other people. They were nothing short of entirely delighted with themselves!

Once she was standing, Breck felt the Highwayman's free arm encircle her waist from behind, pulling her back against his body. He bent, resting his chin on her shoulder for a moment before nuzzling into her neck playfully.

"Come away with me, sweet Breck," the Highwayman whispered. By this time, every patron in Marcelli's large group dining area was staring at the scene. "What say you?" he added, removing his hand from her mouth and letting it rest at her throat.

Breck tried not to giggle, but it was all entirely too wonderful! It was a little more public than she would've perhaps preferred, but wonderful all the same.

"I say, who are you Highwayman?" she said, quoting the book.

"Ah! But that you should know, sweet Breck," the man whispered...

Slowly, Breck began to turn in the man's arms in order to better view the secreted Highwayman of Tanglewood. But suddenly, the lighting in the room burned even more dimly, someone having turned them down. Still, enraptured by the entire event, Breck smiled as she saw she was standing in the arms of a man dressed head to toe in black. A large, draping cowl hung down over his already masked eyes and nose, a flowing cape drooped from his shoulders reaching nearly to the floor. Breck looked down to see that he was indeed wearing black 'breeches' and black boots that cuffed just below his knee. Reaching out she took the silky fabric of his shirt in her hand, unable to believe the perfect detail of his costume. She could hear the repeat of Sherryl's camera shutter clicking away at a mad pace as she tried to imagine who would be willing to involve himself in such an outlandish scheme! The light was too dim and Breck was held too closely in the Highwayman's arms to get a good look at him. Still, his mouth was easily seen and she tried to recognize the grin he wore. But his mustache and goatee hid even the shape of his lips well.

Sherryl was on her feet now, her camera shutter wearing itself out with her maniacal snapping. Breck reached out, running her hands, caressively the breadth of the Highwayman's shoulders. Two could play at this game, and her friends deserved a good show for all their trouble.

Here's what fans are saying about Marcia Lynn McClure:

"Clean, clever and contagious! Marcia Lynn McClure's, *The Heavenly Surrender* stole my heart! This is a book to share, a story to remember and characters that jump off the written page."

"*The Heavenly Surrender* is a wonderful book, a breath of fresh air to society, where respect and love is at the tip of your fingers! I couldn't put the book down; it was so much fun to read and I was sad to finish the book. I can't wait for the next book, but I'm sure it will be worth the wait! Thanks, Marcia! You give life a new meaning!"

Marcia McClure brings the characters alive with her intricately woven plots and romances.

"Her books are so well written they hold you until the last page! She describes the characters so well you think you know them and could jump into their lives. You'll get a little of everything-humor, drama, suspense and, of course, romance! You'll love them!"

"Marcia McClure's work is a delightful contribution to the light-hearted, feel good romance genre. It's the perfect companion to a quiet, relaxing evening. Make plans to turn off the TV, turn on the answering machine, crawl into bed, and enjoy the escape!"

"Marcia's rich imagination serves her well as she weaves her tales and entertains the reader. Her stories are not only a "distraction" from the everyday world, they're also a "great escape" to another time and another place.

"Marcia is a masterful story weaver. Her books have characters that are believable for their human frailties. The plots so intriguing you won't want to put the book down and yet won't want the book to end. Don't stop writing, Marcia!"

"I finished ***Shackles of Honor*** last weekend...my only regret was that the book didn't go on and on! Your gift of writing is my delight and I cherish each story! Thanks for the blessings you bring!"

"I've read all...your books and loved every one of them! In fact, I have reqd them all several times! I love your books and can't wait until your new one comes out!"

"I just finished reading your books. They are awesome! I wanted to thank you for writing great romance that is actually clean!!"

"My mother, sister and I recently read your book, ***The Heavenly Surrender***. We all loved it so much that we went back and read the book severeal times!"

"I just wanted you to know how much I appreciate and enjoy your stories. Your books are practically an answer to my prayer!"

"I couldn't put ***The Visions of Ransom Lake*** down! I took it with me everywhere and read as often as I could!"

"I have finished reading...***Shackles of Honor***r...your writing style had me captured. You have a wonderful way with words...as i wold love to hear this as well if I had written them, that they changed a part of me."

"thank you for the special love stories you share with us that have that special element of romance that makes us remember our own special moments."

"My hubby bought me all of the books he could find of yours, and I read most of them in one weekend! I absolutely love the romance in them!"

"Once I start one of 'Marcia Lynn McClure's' books, I cannot put them down...I love the clean romance and the strong female characters and male characters. I love the passion and the mystery. 'Marcia Lynn McClure' is one of my favorite authors!

ABOUT THE AUTHOR

Marcia Lynn McClure began writing novels as Christmas gifts for her closest friends . . . friends who longed for a breath of the past and missed the romance of bygone eras…friends searching for moments of distraction from the stressful, demanding times in which we live.

Knowing it is the breath of the past and the *"take me in your arms and kiss me"* kind of moments so many women long to relive, Marcia spins her tales of love, life and laughter . . . adventures woven around those compelling, romantic instances which most appeal to a woman's loving heart. Marcia feels that if readers close one of her books with a contented sigh and a delighted smile, feeling rejuvenated, cheerful and uplifted, then she has achieved what she set out to do . . . to shower refreshment and happiness on anyone having experienced the story.

Marcia writes her stories as she gazes out her window into the magnificent beauty of Palmer Lake, Colorado. There she blissfully exists, surrounded by her wonderful husband and three adorable children.

Marcia adores corresponding with her readers. You can write to her at P.O. Box 2055, Ferndale, WA 98248, e-mail her at: marcialmcclure@cs.com, or visit her website, www.marcialynnmcclure.com